Jackie and the

It was almost half past three when we reached the other side of the trees and found that the bridle path didn't leave the spinney where we had expected. Instead it turned up the mountainside.

'Don't you think we ought to go back?' I eyed the rough stony track with misgiving.

'Not to worry,' Babs said. 'The path straightens out when it comes to the shoulder of the hill. It probably leads straight along the ridge before dropping down into the valley.'

'I hope you're right.'

Minute by minute the cloud drifted lower. Soon it was enveloping us and I could no longer see the stream below us, nor the ridge along which Babs had said the path might lead – nothing but a few feet of stony track directly in front and Patch's hindquarters and tail as my cousin rode on into the mist.

I couldn't help thinking that we were well and truly lost.

Also available in the **Jackie** series:

Jackie and the Phantom Ponies

Judith M Berrisford

KNIGHT BOOKS
Hodder and Stoughton

For my young cousin Caroline Fuller and for Tina Jane Lockett, Vivienne Painting, Kate Webster, H. J. Rose and Christopher Dangerfield.

First published in Great Britain in 1979 by Brockhampton Press Ltd

Knight Books edition 1992

British Library C.I.P.
A Catalogue record for this book is available from the British Library.

ISBN 0–340–57547 6

Printed and bound in Great Britain for Hodder and Stoughton Children's Books, a division of Hodder and Stoughton Ltd, Mill Road, Dunton Green, Sevenoaks, Kent TN13 2YA (Editorial Office: 47 Bedford Square, London WC1B 3DP) by Cox & Wyman Ltd, Reading. Typeset by Hewer Text Composition Services, Edinburgh.

Contents

CHAPTER ONE

WE RIDE INTO ADVENTURE

'You're quite sure you two won't get lost?' Mummy paused in giving my pony Misty a farewell pat to look from my cousin Babs to me.

'Of course not,' my cousin assured her. 'We've got the leaflet Carol sent showing the route to the pony stud.'

'In any case, there's a signpost.' I nodded to the pointing arm which read: Stonebeck 5 miles. 'Don't worry, Mummy.' Adjusting the strap of my rucksack, I put my foot in Misty's stirrup. 'You and Daddy had better get going, otherwise you won't reach Newcastle in time to catch the ferry.'

Mummy still looked unreassured. 'I do wish we had time to take you and the ponies right to the farm. If only the wretched petrol pump hadn't become clogged. I'm sure that man from the garage took well over an hour to find us and get the car going again. If only the ferry wasn't sailing three hours early.' She looked anxiously in the direction of Stonebeck. 'It isn't that it would take so long to run you and the ponies to Singing Waters but if we did, we should have to stay and talk to Carol and Mr Browning. We couldn't just drop you and leave. It would be bound to take quite a time.'

'And wouldn't be in the least necessary,' assured Babs. 'Anyway, Jackie and I will enjoy the ride.'

'Come on, dear.' Daddy caught at Mummy's arm, propelling her to the car. 'The girls will be all right, and if we don't move, we shall miss the ferry, and the conference of history lecturers at Copenhagen will find itself without one of its two British delegates.' Half-in and half-out of the car, he paused to look across the roof at Babs and me. 'Now remember, you two — think before you act, be responsible, and don't let Carol down.'

'You can trust us,' I promised.

There was no time to say anything more because, with a twinkle and smile, Daddy slammed the door shut and switched on the engine.

Mummy put her hand out of the other window to wave, and next moment the car was speeding downhill towards the main road, towing the empty trailer behind it.

'That's that, then.' Babs gathered up the reins with a happy smile. 'The start of another adventure.'

'And in a simply super place.'

Touching Misty with my heels I glanced round appreciatively at the green hills and craggy peaks. We were high up on the fells, and below us in the sunlight sparkled the wide stretch of a large lake. The grey stone-built village by the shore and the scattered farmhouses beyond looked like models on a contoured display map. 'I wonder which is Singing Waters?'

'It might be that one.' Babs reined up her skewbald New Forest pony, Patch, and pointed to a cluster of whitewashed buildings nestling in the far valley. Beside the farm we could see a white line of foam where a brook tumbled over the rocks. 'Carol mentioned a stream in her last letter.'

Carol was our eighteen-year-old cousin, Aunt Di's stepdaughter. She'd recently left Stableways, the showjumping establishment run by Aunt Di and Uncle Steve, in order to gain more experience working for a concern that didn't belong to the family. At Singing

Waters she'd found what sounded like the most super job of all time, working on the pony stud run by David Browning – a top-flight showjumper who had twice represented Britain in the European Championships.

Unfortunately his knee had been shattered by a kick and he no longer had enough grip and flexibility to ride. So, as the next best thing, he'd bought the farm and gone in for horse-breeding, crossing fell ponies with thoroughbreds in the hope of getting hunters and jumpers with the brilliance of the sires coupled to the stamina and easy-going temperament of the pony mothers.

Carol had become very enthusiastic about the idea and had written us glowing accounts of the great-hearted fell ponies that could go all day without tiring, climbing the steepest hills and carrying heavy-weight farmers as easily as Patch and Misty carried Babs and me.

'Three cheers for Carol!' Babs seemed to read my thoughts. 'Full marks to her for getting such a fabulous job and for persuading her famous boss to let her invite us up for the Easter holidays to share it.'

For once our ponies did not seem to be echoing our high spirits. Misty is never at her best after a long trailer ride, and what affects Misty usually affects Patch because they're always together. Now both of them were seeming sorry for themselves, dropping their heads and plodding dispiritedly along as if they were feeling the weight of the laden saddlebags and rucksacks, coming on top of the two hundred and eighty miles in the swaying trailer. Both ponies looked as if they were still feeling travel-sick, and I didn't blame them. 'Come on, Misty, cheer up.' I patted her neck before turning to say to Babs. 'What these two need is some green grass under their feet, and a good drink of cold water.'

'The very thing.' My cousin pointed to a bridle path with a sign saying 'Deep Force Falls'. She leaned forward in her saddle to peer down into the valley. 'I'm trying to see where the track leads. It seems to disappear into that woodland.' She pointed with her switch to a fir plantation that made a dark patch on the hill. 'Does it come out again on the other side, that's the question?'

'I think it does.' Following Babs's gaze, I could see a green lane, meandering between grey walls on the far side of the fir trees. 'Let's try it. In any case we've plenty of time. Carol won't be expecting us until teatime.'

Babs nodded. 'It was lucky the ferry people

didn't notify your mother and father about the change in sailing-time soon enough for us to let Carol know that we'd be arriving early.'

The bridle path wandered pleasantly between low stone walls to the mountainside. The turf was bright green from the spring rain and, on either side, the fields were dotted with pale yellow clumps of globe flowers. Young lambs were nuzzling their mothers or skipping about on their spindly black-stockinged legs. The sunshine was warm on our backs, and soon Misty and Patch began to hold their heads higher, looking about them and occasionally flicking back an ear to listen to the bleating sheep.

Deep Force Falls was all we had expected. A hundred feet or more of water, dropping straight as a white horse's tail and misting the air with spray, it plunged into a foaming, fern-fringed pool. We dismounted to let the ponies drink from a calm backwater, then ran our stirrup irons up the leathers, loosened the girths, knotted our reins and let Misty and Patch rest for a while to recover from the journey.

As the ponies cropped the grass, I gathered a bunch of golden kingcups from beside the stream, and Babs took her sketch block from her rucksack and began a drawing of Patch.

After a while we shared some chocolate with the ponies, remounted and trotted towards the fir plantation.

It was almost half past three when we reached the other side of the trees and found that the bridle path didn't leave the spinney where we had expected. Instead it turned up the mountainside.

'Don't you think we ought to go back to the main road?' I eyed the rough, stony track with misgiving.

'Not to worry,' Babs said reassuringly, glancing ahead. 'The path straightens out when it comes to the shoulder of the hill. It probably leads straight along the ridge above the lake before dropping down into the Stonebeck valley.'

'I hope you're right.'

The mountains seemed suddenly dark and menacing now that the sun had gone in. Mist had settled over the higher ground, blotting out the peaks and bringing a chill to the air.

Minute by minute the cloud drifted lower. Soon it was enveloping us and settling in droplets on the ponies' manes. I pulled up the hood of my anorak and shivered. I could no longer see the stream below us, nor the ridge along which Babs had said the path might lead – nothing but a few feet of stony track directly in front and Patch's hindquarters and tail as my cousin rode on into the mist.

I couldn't help thinking that we were well and truly lost.

CHAPTER TWO

GHOST PONIES

'Wait for me,' I called through the mist after my cousin's disappearing back. 'Let's rein up, Babs. The only sensible thing is to dismount, sit down and wait.'

'And perhaps be out on the fell all night, with Carol and David Browning calling out search parties because we haven't turned up?' Babs argued over her shoulder. 'No, Jackie. As long as we can see the track in front of us, we must keep on.'

Telling myself that she might be right, and that as long as we could see the path a little way ahead there was little likelihood of our falling over a precipice, I resigned myself to follow. The cloud was now dense and very wet. The legs of my jeans were soaking and Misty's tack was becoming sodden. The reins felt stiff to my fingers. If only we knew where we were going – or when we might come to a road that would lead us to Stonebeck . . .

I still couldn't help feeling it would be more sensible to turn round and retrace our steps, or rather our hoofprints, but there was no dissuading Babs once she had set her mind to a course of action. I sighed and resigned myself to a long, wet trek.

Oddly enough, Misty did not seem to share my downcast mood. After her long spell in the trailer she had been miserable enough when we set off, but now the mountain air seemed to have perked her up. She played with her bit, eager to get ahead. Patch's pace had also quickened, but he had not left us behind. I could still see his white tail and brown and white quarters. Soon I found I could also see Babs's back. The cloud must be thinning.

Suddenly, out of the mist, came a whinny. Ahead, Patch stretched out his neck to call back. The clouds drifted apart and we saw three ponies, two black and one a very dark dappled brown, deep-chested and sturdy with feathered, miniature Clydesdale legs. They came into view and vanished again, hidden by a drifting scarf of vapour.

Next minute the mist swirled away and we again saw the ponies. They were trotting up the hillside now. A black-and-white sheepdog was loping from side to side at their heels, keeping them together as they went. Where there were ponies and a dog, there would probably be someone driving them. We would be able to ask him the way to Singing Waters. If we hurried we might still arrive in time to stop Carol and her boss panicking because we hadn't turned up.

Babs must have thought the same, because she stood in her stirrups to call. 'Hi! Anybody there? Please can you tell us the way to Stonebeck? We're lost.'

There was no answer. Whether the mist drifted momentarily back across the path, I wasn't sure, but one moment the ponies were there and the next they had simply vanished, the dog with them. The fellside and the path ahead were as bare and empty as if they had never been.

Driving Misty forward, I reined up beside my cousin. 'Where did the ponies go?'

Babs shook her head, as baffled as I was. 'Where can they have gone? There's no cover of any kind. Just the track and the fell.'

I looked around bewildered. 'I've heard of mirages in hot countries but never of one on a damp Westmorland mountainside.'

'It was no mirage, Jackie. There was a man with them. I saw him. He'd gone ahead of the ponies, leaving the dog to bring them on. He must still be somewhere around.' She broke off and then started to shout again. 'Hi, somebody! Help! We're lost.'

From below on the fellside came a whistle.

We looked down to see a dark-haired boy on a peculiarly marked pony – dark brown dappled with black, rather like one of the three ponies we had just seen. As we watched the boy waved and appeared to smile. Then he put his heels to his pony's flanks and came cantering up the steep slope, amid a shower of falling stones.

He reined his pony to a halt beside us. 'Where are you making for?'

'Stonebeck – or at least, Singing Waters, if you know where that is. It's a pony stud,' I told him.

'I know that, right enough.' He gave a friendly grin. 'It's the next farm to ours. It's David Browning's, the showjumper's, place. Everybody round here knows it – leastways everybody that likes ponies, that is. Your best way would be to cut down the hillside to the main road. Tell you what, though, I'll ride along

18

with you.' He turned his mount alongside Misty and Patch.

'That's a kind offer,' I acknowledged. 'But you can't just leave what you were doing and come back with us like that. Weren't you helping to drive the three ponies?'

'What three ponies?' The boy shook his head. 'I wasn't driving any ponies. I was out with Heather Damson for a ride.'

'Heather Damson?' Babs glanced admiringly at the dappled dark brown pony. 'That's a grand-sounding name. I can understand why she's called Damson, but why Heather?'

'She's a rather special pony.' He gave his mount's neck an affectionate pat. 'As a matter of fact, David Browning's been after buying her, but we won't sell. She's descended from a famous stallion, Black Blooming Heather. He belonged to my dad's great-uncle. I'm Graham Wellfield by the way. Anyhow, we want to keep Heather Damson in the family and perhaps breed from her ourselves, if we can find a sire good enough. My dad's very keen on keeping up the quality of the strain.'

'What about one of David Browning's sires?' I queried. 'Wouldn't that do?'

Graham shook his head. 'David's sires are all thoroughbreds. We want to find a dales pony. Dales and fells are practically the same thing.' He looked from me to Babs as he explained, 'But the fells tend to be a bit heavier than the dales. My dad thinks the dales make better riding ponies. The real difference, though, is that the fells belong to this side of the Pennines while the dales originally came from Yorkshire. Dad's great-uncle was a Yorkshireman, you see.'

I nodded. 'I've been admiring Heather Damson's colouring. I've never seen another pony with quite those markings.'

'There aren't many,' Graham said. 'You find them only among dales stock. Fanciers used to call them "Heckberry" on account of their colouring. A heckberry is a kind of whinberry that you find on the moors.'

'One of the three ponies we saw just before we met you was that colour,' Babs told him.

Graham looked puzzled. 'I don't know of any others like Heather Damson round here. They mostly come from the Yorkshire side, you see. Most of the ponies in this district are fells.' He scratched behind his cap with his switch as he looked from Babs to me. 'It's odd that you should have seen those three ponies when I didn't. I was just down the hill and I'd made you out in the mist before you saw me.'

20

'The ponies were there, anyway,' I confirmed. 'Two black, one heckberry, and a dog – a black-and-white sheepdog.'

'There was a man, too,' Babs added. 'I saw him for only a minute and then he vanished.'

'What did he look like?' Graham asked.

'Youngish – tall and stooping,' Babs described. 'He was wearing army surplus denims and a khaki pullover with leather shoulder patches.'

'Funny you should have seen all that when I saw nothing.' I looked at my cousin, suspicious that, with her flare for scenting a mystery, she might have been tempted to dramatise. 'Are you quite sure about the leather patches?'

'Of course.' Babs was quite unperturbed. 'I saw the man quite plainly. He had a beard – a bushy ginger beard.'

Graham laughed. 'I can't think of anyone like that round here. If I didn't know it was only a legend, I should think you'd seen the Ghost Ponies of Borrow Fell.'

'Ghost ponies?' Babs's eyes widened. 'Tell!'

'Well, several times over the last few years, people have reported seeing vanishing ponies on the fells,' said Graham. 'They all say they've had them in view for a few minutes and then they've disappeared. The strange thing is that at least two of the sightings have been on this fellside.'

'On this very hill!' Babs echoed. 'Then they must have been the same ponies that we saw.' She looked across at me excitedly. 'Do you realise what this means, Jackie? We've seen ghosts!'

'I doubt it,' said Graham soberly. 'I hate to disappoint you, Babs, but this is the first time there's been any mention of a ginger-bearded man or a dog with the ghost ponies. There's a lot of cloud on the hills this afternoon. The ponies you saw must have been swallowed up in drifting mist.' He touched Heather Damson with his heels. 'It's after five o'clock so we'd best make top speed; otherwise your cousin, Carol, and David Browning might be setting out to look for you.'

'That would never do,' I said as I put Misty into a canter. 'We don't want to start off on the wrong foot by having them searching for us.'

'You certainly don't.' Above Heather Damson's thrusting shoulders Graham turned from Babs to me. 'David's a stickler for punctuality, so, as he really isn't any too keen on young pony-girl helpers, it's as well for you both to be warned.'

CHAPTER THREE

DANGER FOR BABS

Graham's well-meant warning had a sobering effect. Babs and I renewed our vows to curb our high spirits, to think before we acted, and to be more on our guard than ever not to do anything which might let our cousin Carol down in her employer's eyes.

'Mind you, he can't be all that much down on pony-girls,' Babs tried aloud to persuade herself after Graham had left us at the gate of the well-kept lane leading to the Singing Waters Pony Stud. 'If he was he'd never have agreed to Carol inviting us here.'

'I suppose she's been such a success that he feels any relatives of hers must be equally perfect,' I sighed.

As we rode up the lane towards the farm buildings, ponies came trotting from either side to call to Misty and Patch over the grey stone walls. The lush grass of the valley made ideal grazing and the mares in the fields looked plump and contented as they lifted their inquisitive heads.

The farmhouse itself was square and neat, its blue-painted front door open wide to reveal cosy-looking rugs on the well-polished tiles and a dark oak dresser with blue and white willow-pattern plates. Daffodils bloomed in the beds under the chintz-curtained windows. Around the yard, the stables and cowsheds had been adapted to looseboxes. The crested intelligent head of a grey stallion looked over one of the doors before lifting his lips to call to Misty.

My pony raised her head to whicker back, and next moment a bespectacled boy of about fifteen, dressed in faded corduroys and a leather-patched jacket, came out of the loose-box, carefully closing the door behind him.

'Hello!' He glanced from Babs to me, taking in our rucksacks and saddlebags in surprise. 'I think you must have come up the wrong turning. There's a pony hotel half-a-mile further down the road.'

'But we're not going to the pony hotel,' Babs said blithely. 'We're staying here. We're Carol Rowlands's cousins.'

'Carol's cousins! Jackie and Babs! Whee!'

The boy's expression changed. 'David's going to have something to say about that. Didn't you get our wire?'

'What wire?' I asked with foreboding.

'To tell you not to come. After trying to telephone your number all yesterday evening, David decided to send a telegram to put you off.' Behind his spectacles the boy's grey-blue eyes took on a light of sympathy. 'I'm afraid this is going to come as something of a shock to you both, but the fact is that your cousin Carol was taken ill with appendicitis yesterday afternoon.'

'Poor Carol!' broke in Babs. 'Where is she?' Her colour paled and she turned agitatedly to me. 'We must go and see her right away.'

'There's no cause for alarm.' The boy put up a reassuring hand. 'She had the operation last night and it was quite successful. She's in the hospital at Kendal and doing nicely. As a matter of fact, David's over there visiting her now. He took the other girl groom with him.' He slipped off his spectacles and wiped them carefully, removing a wisp of straw and several specks of dust. 'That's why I'm doing the hay round.'

'Then let us help.' Babs slid to the ground determined to show that we could be useful.

25

'You'll need us more than ever now that Carol's out of action. Just show us where we can turn out Misty and Patch and where to dump our kit, and then we'll lend a hand.'

The boy looked slightly uncomfortable. 'It's a kind and well-meant offer, but I don't think I can. The fact is – this place belongs to my half-brother, David. I'm here for the holidays only because my mama persuaded our mutual father to take her on a package tour to see Rome. My name's Tarquin – I'm named after a Roman King. However— ' he broke off and looked uneasy again. 'That doesn't get us much nearer solving your problem, or does it? Yes, it does!' He was suddenly decisive. 'Blow David! You two have come all this way to spend Easter intending to help with the pony stud, and help you shall. Whatever David says, he can't send you back now.'

'Yippee!' Babs had already unstrapped her saddlebags and dumped them on the ground beside her rucksack. Now she undid Patch's girth and threw it across his saddle. 'Just tell us where to put the tack and the ponies, and we'll pitch right in.'

At Tarquin's suggestion we turned Misty and Patch into a field that had only two other occupants – a stocky young black with a white star, who looked as if he had still to finish growing into his long, slightly hairy legs, and a placid, very plump-looking, dark brown fell mare.

They came trotting to the gate to inspect our ponies. The mare and Patch blew into each other's nostrils, and then began to graze while Misty and the young black stood watching each other, the colt poised uneasily for flight. Then Misty whickered softly to him in a motherly fashion, and he moved gingerly towards her, nose up as though to say: 'I'm only young. Don't hurt me.'

Misty blew again at him reassuringly. They nuzzled each other and then set off round the field at a gallop; the small hooves of my grey Misty thundering beside the hairy soup-plates of the black colt.

'That's that, then. Satisfied?' Tarquin seemed amused that we had to wait to see the ponies settle before throwing ourselves into the chores as promised.

'There's no need to laugh at us,' Babs told him firmly. 'It's important to make sure that there isn't going to be trouble when you introduce strange ponies into a field.'

Tarquin smiled. 'I wouldn't know, I'm afraid,

Babs. I'm not really a pony person. I can about sit on a horse without falling off – any brother of David's would have to – but I don't seem to have the right knack to get any further.'

'We can't all be the same,' I said comfortingly. 'I suppose it depends on where one's main interests lie.'

Babs gave the scholarly-looking boy a friendly smile. 'Never mind, Tarquin, while we're here we'll do our best to win you over to horses.'

'I'm beginning to feel I might like that.' Tarquin wiped his glasses again as he led the way to the feed bins. 'Take Centaur, now – that's the grey I was with when you first saw me – I think I could make a start with him. He's friendly already.'

'Lucky!' I commented as I measured out the horse nuts. 'Not all stallions are.'

'Too right.' Tarquin jerked his head towards the range of looseboxes on the far side of the yard, where a chestnut with a rolling eye was looking out impatiently. 'Saladin, over there can be really treacherous. Apart from David, your cousin Carol is the only one who can do anything with him. He doesn't seem to have taken to the other girl groom at all.'

'In that case,' I said cautiously, 'we'd better leave feeding him until your brother gets back.'

'Nonsense, Jackie.' Babs was walking purposefully across the yard with a sieveful of oats. She spoke back over her shoulder. 'This is where we can really make ourselves useful. If Carol can handle Saladin, there can't be any real vice in him. All he probably needs is kindness and patience . . . There, old boy.' She put up a hand to stroke the arching neck as the crested head bent to lip up the oats. 'Poor Saladin! His net's empty.' She called across to me. 'Come and keep him busy with the oats, Jackie, while I slip inside.'

'I don't think you should— '

Tarquin and I both tried to dissuade her but it was no use. Before we could stop her, thrusting the sieve of oats at me, Babs had lifted the latch and sidled through the half-door. Unconcernedly, the stallion went on lipping up the oats, only by his rolling eye and a slight quiver of an ear, giving any indication that there was a stranger in his box.

Suddenly there came the purr of an engine and the swish of tyres through the puddles as a yellow Jaguar swept into the yard. At the wheel was a sleek blond-headed young man whose face I recognised from newspaper pictures and television shots I had seen.

'My brother, David!' groaned Tarquin. In

his agitation he took off his spectacles to wipe them and cannoned into me, making me drop the sieve.

Cheated of his oats, Saladin snaked his head round to take a piece out of the shoulder of my anorak.

'Look out!' I yelled to Babs, but my cousin had already seen the danger.

She flattened herself against the side of the box as Saladin lashed out with his heels against the manger.

There was the slam of a car door, and David Browning bounded across the yard followed by an auburn-haired girl in an emerald green suit.

'Stand clear, you two.' David Browning flung the command at Tarquin and me as he laid his hand on the loosebox door.

'Don't come in!' In the dimness of the box I could see Babs's face was ashen but she stayed quite still. 'Just talk to him, Mr Browning. I can wait until he quietens down.'

David Browning opened his mouth as if to argue, but something about my cousin's face made him do as she said.

'Here, boy!' He put up a hand to the stallion's neck soothing him, while the auburn-haired girl picked up and passed to him the sieve which still had a few oats clinging to the bottom.

When Saladin was again busy with the oats, Babs slipped out of the loosebox. She stood for a moment in front of David Browning as if expecting to be scolded; then her colour drained completely from her face and she slid to the ground in a faint.

CHAPTER FOUR

A PONY CHALLENGE

Ten minutes later, from the sofa in the farm-house living room where Tarquin had carried her, Babs raised her blue eyes meekly to David's face, while he lectured her.

'Never, never go near either of the stallions unless I'm with you.' Standing in front of the crackling logs in the fireplace, David Browning glanced from my cousin to me. 'That goes for you, too, Jackie – and you, Tarquin. Never any of you, act on your own initiative. I'm the only one who makes decisions at this pony stud, except for Sarah.' He smiled across at the auburn-haired girl who came in from the kitchen with a mugful of hot, sweet tea. 'If I'm not around, you can take your orders from her.'

Sarah Blake paused in the act of handing the mug to my cousin and straightened up to look at her employer sharply.

'Surely you're not going to let these two stay on at Singing Waters? Carol isn't here to look after them and I've got my hands full doing her jobs as well as my own.'

My heart stopped; then beat again in rapid relief as David Browning shrugged. 'Why not? What else can I do? Jackie's parents are on their way to Copenhagen. Babs's are on the Costa del Sol where her father's taken a holiday relief post as padre to one of the English churches. Their Aunt Di has enough to worry about over Carol, and anyway she and her husband have their hands quite full enough with the Easter courses at their jumping establishment, without taking responsibility for this pair of . . . of . . .' He paused and my heart thudded as I waited to hear what condemnatory appellation he thought we deserved. 'This pair of "Pony Nuts"!' he brought out finally. I watched him anxiously as he looked from Babs to me. Was there a twinkle of amusement in his steely blue gaze, or was that merely wishful thinking? He turned again to the auburn-haired girl. 'I'm going to put Jackie and Babs in your charge out of stable hours, Sarah. They can move into the cottage with you, just as they would have done if their cousin Carol hadn't been stricken with appendicitis.'

Carol! For the first time we dared enquire after her condition.

'How is Carol?' I asked anxiously.

'Doing well.' David Browning's face relaxed into a smile, before resuming its stern expression. 'And we'll try to keep it that way, if you don't mind. There's no need to shorten her young life by telling her of Babs's escapade this evening, for instance, or of indulging in any similar foolhardiness in future . . .' His keen gaze searched Babs's face. 'Who did you imagine you were, by the way – the high priestess of horses?'

My cousin had the grace to blush.

'Of course not.' She cast down her eyes. 'I'm sorry. Truly I am, but I thought it would be all right. I thought all Saladin needed was a little understanding.'

'Famous last words,' David said briefly. 'I'm aware that neither you nor Jackie find horses uncomfortable in the middle, as the jokers say, but one thing I would like you to remember while you're here – stallions, especially, can be potentially lethal at either end!'

'What shall we do about supper?'

Babs looked enquiringly at Sarah across the deal-topped table in the cottage kitchen.

Already we had taken our kit upstairs and laid it on the two camp beds in Carol's room.

'Would you like me to get the meal?' I offered, moving towards the pantry where well-stocked shelves of baked beans, corned beef, spaghetti in tomato, and hamburgers were visible through the open doorway.

'Do as you please,' Sarah shrugged. 'Carol's stuff is all on the shelves on the far side of the pantry. There are some sausages of hers in the fridge, and some bacon . . .'

'What about you?' Babs asked in a friendly way. 'We can get your supper ready, too, Sarah, if you like. It would be much easier to prepare one meal for the three of us. For one thing, it would make less washing up.'

'No, thank you.' Sarah's green eyes were cold. 'If your cookery is anything like your pony sense, I don't fancy it – not after this evening's exhibition, at any rate.'

'Don't be like that, please,' I said. 'We couldn't help what happened with Saladin. Babs was only trying to do her best.'

'Then preserve me from her worst.' Sarah raised her eyes to heaven. 'As a matter of fact, if you must know, I'm not eating in the cottage tonight. I'm going over to the farm for supper with David and Tarquin.' She paused and then said meaningly. 'While I'm there, I'm going to try to talk some sense into David Browning's obstinate head. It's quite obvious that he must get another groom. Carol won't be fit for work for weeks.'

'We could do her jobs while we're here,' Babs offered.

'No danger. After what happened with Saladin, David isn't likely to let you within miles of his stock,' Sarah pointed out. 'His are all valuable animals. So I wouldn't unpack anything more than your pyjamas and tooth brushes if I were you. Carol's room will be needed for a new girl, and in any case, I've already got too much to do trying to teach Tarquin to make himself useful without having to act as pony-nurse to you two.' She walked off, leaving Babs and me to prepare our meal.

We had our favourite supper – baked beans, sausages, bacon and fried bread – but in spite of the long day's travelling, we didn't enjoy it much. Sarah's forebodings had dampened our excitement in being at the pony stud, and with what Graham Wellfield had said earlier about David Browning's impatience with zany young helpers, we felt we wouldn't be there long.

'It's odd,' Babs said reflectively, pushing away her plate which still had half-a-round of fried bread and two sausages left on it, 'after what happened with Saladin, I'd have expected David to be angry. He wasn't, though. He was really very kind, in spite of my being idiot enough to faint.'

'Probably that was why.' Try as I might I couldn't find any comfort in the situation. 'Then, too, I suppose he felt he owed it to Carol. She's done very well here so he could hardly turn us out right away with nowhere to go, even though he does think we're a blight.'

'I think there's more to it than that,' Babs said, brightening. 'I've got a feeling David Browning's a bit keen on Carol. Did you notice the way he looked when he was talking about her? There's no doubt her being rushed off to hospital like that has quite upset him. Tarquin told us he'd rung up several times during the day to see how she was, and then he rushed over to Kendal to visit her in hospital as soon as she was allowed visitors.'

'You'd scent a romance anywhere,' I said, eyeing my imaginative cousin fondly.

'Well, sometimes I'm right. It's my belief that David Browning has a very soft spot for Carol, and that's why Sarah is so unfriendly to us.'

'You mean she's jealous?'

'More than likely,' Babs said logically. 'After all any girl of Sarah's and Carol's age who likes horses is bound to admire a handsome showjumping star. Besides which Sarah seems a much tougher sort of person than Carol, doesn't she? She's pretty and all that, but somehow I feel she's had a hard upbringing. She might even hold it against Carol that she's got everything too easily, having a famous National Hunt Jockey father and always having had horses and ponies of her own.'

'It's possible.'

I could see what Babs meant and it made me uneasy because I didn't want our stay at Singing Waters to make things difficult for Carol when she was well enough to return to the stud.

Sarah's disapproving attitude put Babs and me very much on our mettle. We felt it as a challenge to prove our worth as pony helpers, and were determined to make ourselves as useful as possible so as not to give either her or David Browning any further cause for complaint.

I had set the alarm clock for six next morning and by twenty-five past we were washed, dressed, and had downed a mugful of tea and a couple of biscuits each, and were reporting for duty in the stableyard.

Even so, David was before us. As we entered the yard, he was wheeling a barrow of soiled straw from Saladin's box. He paused in his task only to give Sarah instructions.

'Let Babs and Jackie muck out the show-mares' boxes.' He cast a tolerant eye towards the farmhouse where no doubt his half-brother was still asleep. 'I'll take charge of Tarquin when he appears.'

Grudgingly, Sarah introduced Babs and me to the three mares, Stonebeck Bilberry, Stonebeck Blackberry and Stonebeck Bryony, who occupied the looseboxes nearest the house. Bryony and Blackberry were so dark brown as to be almost black while Bilberry was a dark roan with a marked bluey sheen. They stood around thirteen-two hands high with sturdy, feathered legs, flat knees and strong hocks. Their bodies were short with good shoulders and deep barrels. Their heads looked more horse-like than pony, but they had the neat, cat-like ears of Misty and Patch. All three were quiet and good-tempered. They pulled placidly at the hay nets that we gave them while we removed the dirty straw, and barrowed it away before spreading the rest of the bedding to air.

Several times Sarah left what she was doing to supervise us.

'Brush those floors down well. Then fork the bedding over.'

'Hurry up! It's time those three were fed.'

'Don't forget to bring out the water buckets.'

'She's treating us as if we were eight years old,' Babs muttered through clenched teeth.

'Never mind,' I murmured back encouragingly. 'It'll be worth it to stay among all these marvellous ponies.'

While Sarah stood by, directing, we mixed the feeds. As we carried them to the loose-boxes, a loud neighing from the nearest field reminded us that we were very much in sight of Patch. Greedy as always, Babs's pony was letting us know that he was annoyed to see us taking rations to any other ponies.

Suddenly there came the clang of a metal gate against its post followed by a clatter of hooves as Misty and Patch cannoned into the yard. At the same moment came a thin, frightened pony squeal.

'The colt!' Babs and I dropped the feed buckets and almost collided as we raced to the field.

CHAPTER FIVE

A MISSING MARE

A piteous sight met us.

There was the gate, tilted and half-off its hinges, while the leggy black colt stood trembling and trapped. One of its large, feathered hooves was wedged in the angle of the ironwork.

As we ran, we could see blood welling from a deep gash in his fetlock as the colt struggled to pull his hoof free.

'Steady, boy.' Babs reached him a few seconds ahead of me. 'Stand still; Jackie, help me to hold him! He'll break his leg if he struggles like this.'

From the farmyard came the rattle of buckets and Misty's indignant whinny as Sarah tried to shoo her and Patch away from the scattered pony nuts.

'Come quickly! Sarah! Mr Browning!' I yelled. 'Help!'

David Browning was on the scene in a matter of seconds.

'Ebony! Steady boy!' He spoke quietly to the colt, his hand on its neck, while he sized up the problem. 'Babs, run and tell Sarah to bring a hacksaw.'

He took my cousin's place, using all his strength to restrain the colt.

Ebony still squealed and tossed his head, at the same time trying to tug his hoof free.

It must have been only a couple of minutes, although it seemed like hours, before Babs and Sarah returned with the hacksaw. David signalled them to keep quiet but Sarah was unable to contain her scorn.

'More trouble!' she scoffed. 'And for Ebony, too. Poor David! It seems as if your kind heart's led you to take in a couple of real jinxes.' Her expression changed to one of heartfelt sympathy. 'The first colt of your own breeding! The hope of the stud! And this has to happen.'

She bent to use the hacksaw, but her wrist was not strong enough.

David motioned to Babs and me. 'You two take over here. Keep Ebony still and talk to him calmly while I saw through the metal.'

The colt was free and David was leading him towards the stables to attend to his injured fetlock when Tarquin appeared, looking sleepy as he emerged from the farmhouse to join us.

'All you energetic people, up and about the stables at the crack of dawn! When I see you all hard at work so early in the morning, I wonder what hope there is for a lazybones like me to make any progress with horses.'

His elder brother cocked a humorous eyebrow at him. 'Well, Tarquin, if you will burn the midnight oil! I daresay the rest of us were all tucked up in our beds and dreaming while you were still struggling with your studies.'

Tarquin looked apologetically from Babs to me. 'It sounds as if I'm an awful swot, but I've got my GCSEs at the end of the summer term.'

'Tarquin's a year ahead of his age group,' David explained. 'He's the brains of the family in fact.' He gave Ebony a pat before turning to Sarah. 'Be an angel and fetch the anti-tetanus and antibiotic injection packs from the tack room.'

Once she had gone his chatty manner dropped and he fixed Babs and me in turn with a steely gaze.

'In my experience most young pony-girl

43

helpers are a menace, but you two take the biscuit! Two major disasters in less than twelve hours. I don't know how you do it.'

'We didn't,' I began. 'At least, we didn't get the gate off its hinges, although I suppose we must take the blame for having two such greedy and unruly ponies as Misty and Patch.'

'Even they couldn't have managed to break the gate down,' said David. 'But what I want to know is how you came to put them with Ebony and Elderberry in the first place? Of all the grazing available, why did you have to choose that particular field, with my most promising young colt and a mare about to foal?'

'That was my fault, David.' Tarquin removed his glasses and began to polish them nervously as he faced his elder brother. 'Like the clot I am where ponies are concerned, I thought Ebony's field would be the best because it had only two occupants.'

David looked at him, as if he was counting up to ten, but all he said was: 'Let this be a lesson to you, all of you.' He included Babs and me. 'It just goes to show that I'm right when I ask you never to act on your own initiative. The obvious thing would have been to put Misty and Patch into two of the empty looseboxes where they couldn't do any harm, until I got back and could deal with things.' He looked from my cousin to me as though we were a major worry and I knew that Babs was crossing her fingers just as I was and hoping that he wouldn't decide to send us away. 'For Carol's sake, I'd like to keep you here, and for your own sakes, I'd like you to be able to feel you were being useful, but – and this is a big "but" – I can't afford any more mistakes. So from now on, ask first and act afterwards, understood?'

'Understood!' we promised.

David held out his hand as Sarah came back with the syringes.

'Give me the antitet jab first, and the antibiotic afterwards.' He motioned to me. 'Jackie, take Ebony's head.'

Moving as quietly as possible I took David's place beside the colt. My right arm was across his neck and my left hand stroked his nose while David prepared to give the injections. Nothing like this had ever happened to the colt and we all held our breath to see how he would take it, as David deftly and quickly plunged the needles first into one side of his neck and then the other.

To our relief, Ebony never flinched, merely rolling his eyes enquiringly from one to the other of us as if wondering why he was getting all the attention.

It wasn't until the wound on the colt's fetlock had been washed with salty water and we had put down clean straw for his bedding that anybody realised there was something still amiss.

'Put Misty and Patch in the bottom field with the four fell mares,' David instructed Babs and me, before turning to his half-brother. 'Tarquin, fetch the screwdriver and a hammer from the tack room. We'd better fix the gate before Elderberry gets out.'

'Elderberry?' Babs and I looked at each other uneasily. There had been no other pony in the field when we went to Ebony's aid and we wondered how to break the bad news that Elderberry had got away.

Babs drew a deep breath. 'The mare isn't in the field, David. She was there last night when we turned Misty and Patch in with her and the colt, but I'm sorry to have to tell you that she wasn't there when we went to rescue Ebony just now.'

David looked at her as if he couldn't believe the bad news.

He turned to Sarah. 'Didn't you put Elderberry in the stables when you caught Misty and Patch?'

She shook her head. 'I haven't seen the mare this morning.'

'Then she must have broken out first and wandered away.' David's face was serious. 'Elderberry's due to foal any day now. We don't want her straying about the fells in all weathers. We must find her quickly and get her back to the farm before she wanders too far.' He turned to Babs and me. 'You two saddle your own ponies. Sarah, take Centaur. Tarquin?'

He turned to his younger brother who hooked his spectacles firmly behind his ears and looked suddenly business-like. 'As long as someone will give me a hand to catch her, I'll be all right on Romany.'

'And I'll take Saladin.' David strode decisively towards the tack room. 'Everybody carry a spare halter. Bring your mounts into the yard as soon as you've saddled up and I'll tell you in which direction to search. We'll have to split up if we're to have any hope of covering the area.'

CHAPTER SIX

MYSTERY ON THE FELLS

Sheep were bleating in the fields below when Misty and I rode up the path towards High Tarn.

Down in the valley, Patch's white markings showed up in the sunlight as Babs trotted him towards the village.

Away to the right, Sarah and the grey Centaur, were already on the skyline while, two fields to the left, Tarquin was dismounting from the sensible Romany to lead her through a stubborn gate.

Glancing back over my shoulder, I saw David fighting Saladin as the stallion tried to buck his way through a tide of golden daffodils at the lakeside.

It was a perfect morning. Curlews bubbled in the blue sky overhead. The scent of crushed thyme rose from the turf below

Misty's hooves. The creak of saddlery was music as we cantered, and my pony shook her head protestingly against the bit as I slowed her deliberately to a walk.

'It's all very well,' I patted her. 'I enjoy taking the tickle out of your hooves as much as you do, but we're not out for pleasure this morning, Misty. This is serious. Elderberry might stray high up the mountain. There could be a sudden snowstorm tonight, and her foal might be born and die from exposure if we didn't find her. It's important to go slowly so that we can have a thorough look round.'

Leaving the path, I rode across to a barn that stood open on the hillside. This was the kind of place for which David had said the missing pony might make. She could be looking for feed or seeking somewhere quiet and safe to have her foal.

I dismounted to look inside, but Elderberry wasn't there. Swinging myself back into the saddle, I trotted across the field to examine a wide clump of gorse.

Looking into hollows and gulleys, behind walls and thorn trees, I made my way up the mountainside. On the way I met a party of booted walkers coming down from the peak. They had spent the night on the mountain to see the sunrise. They said it had been bitterly cold up there and they had been glad of their padded sleeping bags. No, they hadn't seen a very plump pony. In fact they hadn't seen any ponies at all since yesterday afternoon when they'd booked in at the Youth Hostel. They'd seen a brown pony then. In fact there had been two browns and another pony, very dark and queerly marked.

'It was sort of mottled black and brown,' said a youth with longish, fair hair who seemed to be the leader of the party.

The three ponies that Babs and I had seen yesterday afternoon when we'd been lost in the mist!

'Was anyone with them?' I asked.

The longish-haired youth nodded. 'A big fellow, rather thin and stooping a bit. He had a ginger beard.'

'Did you notice what he was wearing?'

'Fawn denims,' said another youth.

'And a khaki pullover with leather shoulder patches,' a girl added.

'There was a dog, too,' said the first youth. 'A black-and-white sheepdog. I noticed, because he kept chivvying the ponies as if he was driving sheep.'

I nodded.

So Babs had been right in her description of the man and dog. One thing was certain – the disappearing ponies of yesterday afternoon had been real, solid flesh and not mere phantoms. This time, at least 'Ghost Ponies of Borrow Fell' were fact, not legend, but how was that to help us in finding the missing Elderberry?

Stopping to search every likely spot on the way, it took me nearly an hour to come within sight of High Tarn.

The small lake lay dark and mysteriously deep in a steep-sided hollow between two peaks. I rode close, looking for hoofprints on the fine shale at the water's edge. Nothing grew there but ferns and a stunted birch tree, and, at first, I could see no sign of a pony. Then, as I rode round, I noticed the prints of an unshod pony on some soft ground at the far end of the lake where a stream trickled in from the mountain.

The hoof marks stopped at the water's edge as though the pony had gone there to drink. They were bigger than Misty's, and I thought they must belong to the missing Elderberry. I cast about for more in the hope that they might indicate which way the pony had gone.

I found none, and I realised that the mare

must have emerged on to a solid slab of rock. Most of the ground around was soft and I knew it would be only a matter of time before I would find more hoof marks. I was still searching when I heard a frantic whinny – the unmistakable sound of a pony in trouble.

Putting my heels to Misty's sides, I drove her up the gully at a canter. We emerged between the sides of the two peaks to find ourselves on the flattish moorland of the high fell.

Reining up, I looked round, but I could not see any pony. The whinny sounded again, thinner and more despairing. It seemed to come from a dark patch of ground a quarter of a mile away. Shading my eyes with my hand against the sun I could just make out the head and about half the body of a pony. It looked as if it was up to its knees in a bog!

Thankful that I had a halter rope, and with no very clear idea of what I intended to do – I urged Misty into a gallop.

As spurts of heather and gorse flew from my pony's pounding hooves, I heard a shout from behind me. It was a boy's voice, and for a moment, I thought Tarquin, having drawn a blank on the lower slopes, had followed me up to the tarn. Glancing back, I yelled over my shoulder:

'Emergency! Can't stop! Come and lend a hand!'

The boy waved to show that he understood, but there was no gleam of spectacles reflecting in the sunlight, and his mount looked smaller and darker than Romany. Looking back again as he settled down to ride, I realised that the boy was not Tarquin but Graham Wellfield. I felt oddly comforted. I liked Tarquin but, as he himself admitted, he was not a country person and no pony expert whereas Graham was a farmer's son and had an inborn knowledge of the fells.

Heather Damson was bigger than Misty, but my pony had the speed, so I arrived first on the scene. Halter rope in hand, I slid to the ground and started to pick my way over firm tussocks to the pony.

'Hold hard, Jackie!' Graham shouted, as he pounded up behind. 'It's no use rushing into action before we've sized things up. You'll only get yourself bogged, too.'

Meanwhile the trapped pony, with the good sense of her breed, stayed quiet. Probably she realised that to plunge and struggle would only trap her further in the mud. As it was, the awareness of her placid eyes watching us trustingly spurred us to think quickly what we could do to help.

'Give me that halter, Jackie.' Graham slipped another from his saddle flap and knotted it skilfully to mine to make about fifteen feet of 'rope'. 'It's a good thing David told you to carry this. You never know when it will be needed. All kinds of pony emergencies happen up here on the fell.' He completed a fisherman's knot and tested it to make sure that it would take the strain before fastening the improvised rope to Heather Damson's girth. 'You're a lighter weight than I am, Jackie. Do you think if you take off Misty's surcingle you can manage to get across the bog to pass it round the mare?'

Gingerly I balanced from tussock to tussock. The bogged mare whickered as I reached her side, and I spoke to her soothingly. Then Graham passed me his jacket.

'Spread it out to take your weight.' He insisted as I demurred. 'Don't worry about the jacket, I daresay it will clean, and, in any case, Mother will understand. She's sometimes had to help get ponies out of bogs herself before now. It's a part of everyday life on the fells.'

With the jacket beneath me, I spread-eagled

myself across the tussocks. Luckily the pony had still not sunk much beyond her knees and her chest was clear of the mud, so I was able to get Misty's surcingle around her barrel. Then I looped through the end of the halter rope.

'Try to ease the mare out while Damson and I tug.' Graham mounted his pony and slowly rode her forwards to take the strain.

She seemed to know what was wanted and I could well believe that she had done this kind of thing before. Digging in her toes and heels she hauled the halter ropes tight while I lifted the helpless pony as well as I could. There were grunts from Heather Damson, encouragements from Graham and heavy breathing from me. Finally there was a sucking noise and the trapped pony began to help herself by dragging her own limbs free. Within five minutes she was on firm ground, shaking huge clots of sour-smelling bog from her coat while I brushed it from my jeans. To my surprise my legs were trembling, and my knees felt weak.

'Are you sure you're O.K., Jackie?' Graham dismounted and came to see how I was bearing up before trying to beat the caked mud from his jacket.

'I think so,' I said shakily. 'But it was a good thing you came along, Graham, otherwise

Elderberry might have drowned in the bog before I could get her free.'

'Elderberry?' Graham looked puzzled. 'Why do you call the mare that? She's not David Browning's Elderberry.'

'Then whose is she?' I felt baffled. I'd seen Elderberry for only a few minutes when Babs and I had turned Misty and Patch into the field the previous evening, and, to me, many of the fell ponies were so similarly marked that she still looked like her.

I told Graham briefly what had happened and how the mare came to be missing.

'So the gate was partly off its hinges?' Graham whistled. 'Sounds fishy! The strange thing is that Dad's also lost a brood mare. That's why I'm up here. We're both on a similar quest.'

I glanced at the dark brown pony who, having shaken off the worst of the mud, was now pulling unconcernedly at the grass.

'I wonder whose she can be?'

Graham shook his head. 'I haven't the faintest idea.' He walked across to inspect the mare more closely. 'I've never seen her before so the mystery deepens. She's not a local and that's for sure.'

CHAPTER SEVEN

WHOSE PONY?

Graham separated the halters and slipped one over the brown pony's ears before opening her mouth to look at her teeth.

'I thought so,' he said presently. 'She's just a young filly. She's only got her first two permanent teeth.'

'So she's three years old.' I peered at the two strong new teeth in the centre of the pony's jaw amid the worn-down milk teeth. 'That should simplify matters. We'll be able to find out from the police whether anyone has reported a three-year-old, dark brown fell filly as missing.'

'If she is a fell?' Graham's brow knitted. 'She could be a dales. She's a bit lighter in build than most of the fell ponies round here.'

'Like Heather Damson.' I could see a similarity in build between the filly and Graham's pony. 'By the way, I had news of the other heckberry and the two dark brown ponies that Babs and I saw in the mist yesterday.' I related what the sunrise-viewing walkers had said.

'Sounds interesting,' Graham commented. 'It seems as though there may be several strange ponies wandering around just now.' He put his foot into Heather Damson's stirrup, bringing the filly alongside by her halter rope as he mounted. 'We'd best get down to Singing Waters and compare notes with David. If Elderberry hasn't been found and nobody's come across Dad's mare while they have been searching, I shall begin to believe there are pony thieves at work.'

'Do you mean Elderberry could have been stolen?' I paused, horrified, in mounting Misty.

Graham nodded as he put the filly's halter rope among his reins. 'This pony may also have been stolen but managed to escape.'

'And the other two ponies that Babs and I saw yesterday,' I mused as I touched Misty into a trot. 'If all three were stolen as well as your dad's brood mare, it would seem there may be quite a sizeable pony rustling operation under way.'

'Could be,' said Graham. 'Some of them may have been driven over the Pennines from

Yorkshire. The thieves may be collecting a large batch for shipment . . .'

'Not for horsemeat?' I shuddered.

Graham shook his head. 'Pure bred fell and dales ponies are too valuable for that. It's more than likely the thieves would be collecting a batch to send across the Atlantic. Fell mares and fillies would fetch high prices in America. It's my belief we're on to something big.'

As we sat round eating a snack lunch in the Singing Waters kitchen before setting off to continue our search, David Browning was inclined to agree with Graham's reasoning.

'The fact that there are five ponies already involved makes me think it's a well-planned operation.' Mug of coffee still in his hand, he moved across to the telephone. 'I'm going to report it all to the police.'

Munching our bread, cheese and tomatoes, the rest of us watched while he dialled the number of the police station and asked to speak to the sergeant on duty.

'Good afternoon. This is David Browning of Singing Waters Pony Stud. I want to report one of my mares as missing . . . What? You've had three other animals reported strayed this morning? Were they all fell ponies? They were.

Can you tell me then whether they included one belonging to Mr Wellfield? No. Then you can add another to the list. That will make five. Descriptions? . . . Mine was a dark brown, five-year-old mare due to foal any day . . . The Wellfields'?' He turned to Graham. 'What colour was your pony?'

'Dark grey, black near hind, light mane and tail, well-feathered. Thirteen-one hands high.' Graham paused between each detail for David to pass on the information to the police sergeant.

'Right?' David continued. 'Got that have you, Sergeant? Well, now I'd better give you the description of the pony which one of my helpers found bogged this morning. It's a three-year-old filly, dark brown, just under thirteen hands, with a black mane and tail . . . Yes, that's the trouble. These fells do all look so much alike don't they? You'll instruct your men to keep a lookout? Good! I wonder then whether you could alert the police in the port areas to keep watch for any ponies awaiting shipment. If they have all been stolen, it must be a well-organised crime. I would say there would almost definitely be some attempt to get them out of the country. The thieves couldn't hope to get away with selling them here. Too many of us would be on the lookout.' He paused and we could hear an emphatic crackle as the sergeant replied. 'You don't agree? There are plenty of small breeders who might not be too particular? You may be right, of course, Sergeant, but I'd feel happier if you'd get them to watch out for any attempt at shipment, just the same.'

He put down the telephone and turned to face us with a sigh.

'I think that police sergeant imagines we're being overdramatic.'

'But he will instigate a watch on the ports?' Tarquin asked anxiously.

'He said that he would, but you know how it is.' David spread his hands in a gesture of defeat. 'There are so many fishing harbours along this coast and so many small vessels using them.'

'All the more reason why we must find the ponies before the thieves have time to get them to a ship.' Babs took her plate and mug to the sink. 'Come on, everybody, bring me your crockery. The sooner we get the washing up done, the sooner we can get out again and carry on with the search.'

'Where is there left to look?' Sarah straightened the auburn sweep of her hair in front of the mirror. 'If you ask me, the police sergeant is right.' Her face took on an expression of adult wisdom as she gazed round at Babs, Tarquin, Graham and me before turning to David. 'They've all been reading too many pony stories and seeing too much television. Don't you think that's possible, David?'

'I don't know what to think.' David picked up his switch from the dresser and turned to the door. 'But I do know that I don't want Elderberry foaling out on the fell. I'm off to saddle Saladin again. The rest of you, leave those dishes to soak, and get your ponies ready. I want the countryside combed within a five-mile radius. Domestic chores can wait. Perhaps Elderberry won't.'

Tracing and retracing our mounts' tracks of the morning, we carried out an even more thorough search. Sometimes singly, and sometimes in pairs, we split up to quarter various areas, reporting back to whatever point David had nominated as a rendezvous, but entirely without success. Both Elderberry and the Wellfields' dark grey mare seemed to have vanished without trace.

'What now?' Tarquin asked at half past five as we met by the jetty at the Stonebeck end of Bright Water. 'I'm famished. Romany's almost too tired to put one hoof in front of the other and we're no nearer getting the missing ponies back than we were this morning.'

'Goodness knows.' David checked Saladin who now seemed as glad as the others of an excuse for a break. 'The only sensible thing would be to go back to the farmhouse to eat.' He glanced towards Babs and me. 'Do you think you two can rustle up a meal for us all? Take whatever you like from the refrigerator and the pantry and have it on the table by half past six. Meanwhile the rest of us will keep on with the search.'

As Babs and I turned our ponies homewards, Graham Wellfield trotted after us.

'I'll come with you.' He reined Heather Damson alongside Misty. 'For one thing I must telephone home to let my mum and dad know where I am. For another, I want to see just how Elderberry got out of that broken-hinged gate.'

Twenty minutes later, back at Singing Waters, Babs and I were unsaddling Misty and Patch while Graham gazed in a puzzled way at the still lopsided metal gate.

He dismounted from Heather Damson and, looping her reins over his arm, went to inspect the buckled hinge more closely.

'Do you know whether David had a go

at mending this?' he asked a few seconds later.

I shook my head. 'He intended to. In fact he'd asked Tarquin to fetch the tools to help him—'

'But then we discovered Elderberry was missing,' Babs put in. 'So, of course, we had to drop everything and saddle up to look for her.'

'So the gate wasn't touched by anyone here?' Graham looked from Babs to me for confirmation. 'In that case it must be a pony thief who got it off its hinges. This couldn't have been done by a pony.' He pointed to the buckled metal and damaged paint.

'It looks as if someone had a go at it with a hammer,' said Babs.

'Quite,' Graham nodded. 'It's odd that none of you heard it. The thief must have made quite a noise.'

'It's some distance from the farm,' Babs pointed out, 'and we were so tired last night that it would have taken an earthquake to waken us.'

'I did wake up once in the night,' I said. 'It was in the middle of a heavy shower and I heard the rain spattering outside the window.'

'There was thunder about, too,' Graham

remembered. 'I suppose that would disguise any noise made by the thief.'

At that moment there came the ring of horseshoes on the stony lane and we looked round to see Sarah and Centaur trotting fast up the lane.

'Still gossiping?' she called to us as she turned into the yard. 'I thought you two were supposed to be getting tea ready. You'll have to get a move on if David's going to drive us into Kendal to see Carol. The hospital doesn't allow any visitors after seven-thirty.'

CHAPTER EIGHT

BABS ON THE TRAIL

As things turned out Babs and I had to make our own way to the hospital to visit Carol.

While he and David were still searching for the missing mare, Tarquin spotted the prints of an unshod pony in a muddy lane not far from Singing Waters. So, hoping that this time they really were on Elderberry's trail, the two brothers returned to the farmhouse only to wolf down bacon and eggs before setting off to continue the search.

Babs and I offered to go with them, but David wouldn't hear of it.

'No. You two must visit Carol. She'll be expecting someone. Don't tell her anything about Elderberry being missing or she'll start to worry. Hurry, now. You'll just have time to catch the twenty to seven bus from the crossroads. Here . . .' He paused to take a paperback book from the shelves and hand it to us. 'Give her this; it's the story of a year in the life of a fell farmer, so I know she'll enjoy it. Tell her I'll be in to see her tomorrow.'

So, snatching up our shoulder bags, Babs and I had to hurry off just as we were, muddy, untidy and smelling of horse, leaving Sarah, David, Graham and Tarquin wearily to ride away to continue the quest.

We found Carol sitting up in bed looking pale but not too ill. As she saw us coming down the ward towards her she smiled, but her eyes seemed to stray beyond us as if she was looking for someone else.

'David couldn't get away,' I said quickly. 'He'll be coming tomorrow. Meanwhile he's sent you this.'

Carol forced another smile as she took the book. It was as if she was trying not to show her disappointment that David was not there in person. 'It's just as well really, I suppose. It will give the three of us a chance to have a good talk . . . Now, tell me all you've been doing and what you think of Singing Waters.'

'Tell us first how you feel,' I said, knowing that it was going to be difficult to satisfy her curiosity about our doings at the pony stud without letting slip any information that might lead her to deduce that something was amiss.

'Rather as if I've been kicked by a pony in the stomach,' Carol said wryly. 'Otherwise not too bad. When I got out of bed for a few minutes this afternoon, my legs felt like jelly but the nurses say that will pass. By tomorrow I should be a lot better, I expect.' She looked from Babs to me questioningly. 'Something's wrong isn't it?'

'Whatever makes you think that?' Babs tried to be airily noncommittal.

Carol held up the *Year In the Life of a Fell Farmer* and smiled.

'Just that I've read this twice already as David would know perfectly well if he hadn't been too preoccupied to remember. Something happened at the last minute to prevent him coming, didn't it? So he sent the book to let me know that he was thinking of me. Tell me what's wrong at the stud? Is it Saladin?'

'You're being fanciful,' I hedged.

Babs's eyes met mine across the bed. 'It's no

use, Jackie. We'll have to tell her. If we don't, she'll only imagine the worst.'

'Too right,' Carol nodded. 'Come on, now. Let's have it.'

'I only hope we've done right,' I said doubtfully when Babs and I left the hospital gates twenty minutes later. 'I hope Carol isn't going to lie awake worrying about Elderberry.'

'Worrying about David, more like,' Babs said smiling. 'She's almost as smitten as he is, don't you think?'

'I think she *likes* David,' I said cautiously. 'Knowing Carol I don't expect she'll let it develop into anything more for quite a while. She's got too much sense to enter into any romantic involvement before she's finished her training.'

'Come off it, Jackie. Carol's eighteen-and-a-half,' Babs pointed out. 'And people don't always let their heads rule their hearts. Circumstances alter cases, as is well known. With David breeding showjumpers and Carol a first-class rider to take them into the ring, I think it is a very suitable match. I wouldn't be at all surprised if they didn't get engaged . . .'

I was only half-listening to Babs's romantic speculations because we were still a good distance from the bus stop. My watch said seven-thirty five and I knew that the bus to Stonebeck was due at twenty-to-eight.

'Come on.' I tugged at my cousin's sleeve. 'We'll have to run or we'll miss the bus.'

'Just a minute, Jackie.' Babs shook off my hand and we came to a sudden halt. 'Look!'

'There's no time to linger.' I caught at the strap of her shoulder bag.

Babs dug in her heels. 'On the other side of the road. Don't you see?' She jerked her head across the street to where a tall young man with a stoop was walking rapidly in the opposite direction.

'Red beard.' I mentally checked the young man's appearance with my cousin's description of the man whom she said she had seen driving the ponies through the mist the previous afternoon. 'Khaki denims . . .'

'And I bet he's got a leather-patched, army-surplus sweater under that donkey jacket.' My cousin caught my arm as she stared after him. 'He's stopped at the other bus stop. We must wait and see where he goes.'

'And miss our own ride home?' I queried. 'Babs, we can't; David will go mad.'

'It's in David's interests that we find out where the pony thief is going,' Babs argued.

'Anyway, there's sure to be another Stonebeck bus later on, and this is too good a chance to miss. If we follow Redbeard he may lead us to the stolen ponies.'

Against my better judgment, I allowed myself to be persuaded.

We lingered as if we were looking into the window of a flower and fruit shop which was conveniently situated for friends and relatives visiting patients in the hospital.

'If we'd been earlier we could have bought something here to take to Carol.' My attention was almost entirely diverted by the tempting display.

'Never mind,' consoled Babs. 'There's always tomorrow. If we pool our pocket money we can take her one of those super baskets of fruit.'

'Peaches, grapes – the lot,' I nodded, trying not to allow myself to be abstracted by the sight of the Stonebeck bus drawing up across the road.

'Just look at those tulips . . .' Babs was putting on an act for the benefit of Redbeard who was waiting by the Black Water bus stop.

'And the roses.' I tried to throw myself equally into the part although I couldn't help watching the Stonebeck bus drive away and wondering what time the next one would leave.

Just then a faded blue cattle truck rattled down the street, and, from the corner of my eye, I saw Redbeard thumb it to a stop.

'Look!' I dragged at Babs's arm. 'Or rather, don't look now, but Redbeard isn't going to travel by bus after all. He's getting a lift.'

'Blow!' said Babs. 'We've missed our bus for nothing. Now we shan't be able to see where he's going. But never mind.' She brightened and turned openly to look as the cattle truck drove off. 'Did you see what I saw? The name of the owner was painted on the side.'

'George Clutterbuck. Cattle and General Transport. Lake Garage, Black Water,' I reported. 'That could give us a real lead. Did you see how the driver greeted Redbeard?'

'Very matey,' Babs nodded. 'Almost as if he'd been looking out for him in fact.'

'Quite,' I agreed. 'That might be the very truck which they've been using to transport the ponies.'

'Could be,' Babs said. 'All the same, don't let's get carried away, Jackie. It wouldn't do for us to go haring off to Black Water now. Even if Redbeard and his pal have got the ponies there, there's not much you and I could do on our own against a couple of men. Our best course is to go back to Singing Waters and report it all to David.'

CHAPTER NINE

STOLEN BY NIGHT

A few minutes later we were studying the timetable on the board by the bus stop.

'There's nothing here after twenty-to-eight.' Babs ran her finger down the Stonebeck column.

'Then we've missed the last bus. What do we do now?'

We faced each other in dismay. At the back of our minds was a vision of David, Tarquin and Sarah returning from a fruitless search for Elderberry only to find that we, too, were missing.

'We'll have to phone.' Babs pulled open the door of the kiosk by the bus stop.

We could hear the telephone bell ringing at Singing Waters, but nobody lifted the phone to reply which meant that David and the others must still be out looking for the mare. So there was no question of anyone coming to meet us with the car. Both Babs and I had often been warned of the dangers of hitch-hiking and our parents had made us promise never to accept lifts from strangers, so that left us only one course of action. Telling ourselves that we were not really as tired as all that, and that walking would make a pleasant change after a long day in the saddle, we set off to trudge the five miles to the pony stud.

We hadn't gone far, however, when a muddy-looking Range Rover pulled up ahead of us and a dark-haired, slight-built man, with a farmer's weather-beaten face and an unmistakable likeness to Graham Wellfield, leaned out.

'I suppose you two girls haven't seen a straying pony anywhere along this road, have you?'

'A grey mare?' Babs shook her head.

'How do you know it was a grey mare that I was looking for?' For a moment the farmer's brow knitted in puzzlement. Then he laughed. 'Of course. The penny's dropped! You must be the two young ladies who've come to stay at Singing Waters. My son, Graham, was talking about you. David Browning's also lost a mare, hasn't he? You've been out looking for it all day, I suppose.'

'That's right.'

We told Mr Wellfield how David had sent Babs and me into Kendal to visit Carol in hospital and about the truck we had seen pick up the red-bearded man at the bus stop.

'Here, wait a minute. It sounds like a detective story,' Mr Wellfield exclaimed. 'I've known Clutterbucks for years. I can tell you there's nothing fishy about them. They run an honest transport business . . . Still, as you missed the bus through trying to watch our pony interests, the least I can do is to give you a lift home.' He opened the door of the Range Rover for us to climb in. 'I'd just like to run up to the Dawsons' farm first. I bought the mare from them, so it's possible she may have made her way back.'

The Wellfields' pony was not at the Dawsons' farm, but still Graham's father would not take our theory about the thieves seriously. 'Our Graham had the same sort of idea.' He laughed. 'He said he thought that the gate of the Singing Waters field had been knocked off its hinges by a thief with a hammer. I reckon the only knock that gate received came from the hooves of one of the ponies. Stray ponies are one of the facts of a fell farmer's life. It doesn't take pony thieves to help them go missing.' He chuckled. 'All you young people are the same these days. Fanciful!

It comes from all the serials about police work that you see on the telly.'

We realised it was no use arguing, so we thanked Mr Wellfield for the lift and got him to drop us at the bottom of the Singing Waters lane. Babs and I both felt it was going to be hard enough convincing David of the logic of our conclusions about Redbeard and his friend without Graham's father casting added doubt.

A light was burning in the farm kitchen when we reached the door, but David and Tarquin were not there, only Sarah who turned from the soup she was stirring to greet us angrily.

'And just what do you think you've been doing, missing the last bus to Stonebeck with never a word to anyone to let us know where you were?'

'We tried to telephone,' I said.

'You tried to telephone!' Sarah scoffed. 'And when you got no reply I suppose it didn't occur to you to go on trying. Oh, no! You had to make your own way back here. Didn't you even stop to think that David and Tarquin and I would be worried? How did you get back, anyway, not hitch-hike, I hope?'

'Of course not.' Babs explained how Graham's father had given us a lift.

'Where are David and Tarquin?' I asked. 'Surely they're not out looking for us?'

'How did you guess?' Sarah asked with heavy sarcasm. 'At this moment they're driving to Kendal, hoping to pick you up en route. What puzzles me is how neither you nor Mr Wellfield saw them. A yellow Jaguar isn't something one can easily overlook.'

'We must have missed them when Mr Wellfield drove up to the Dawsons' farm.' Babs looked at me unhappily. 'Oh dear, Jackie. What are we going to say to David when he gets back?'

'You won't be saying anything – not tonight, anyway.' Sarah pushed us firmly towards the door. 'Both David and Tarquin will have had quite enough for one day – searching first for Elderberry, and then you. The best thing you can do is to go across to the cottage, get your supper, and go to bed. I'll explain to David and Tarquin what happened while they're having their soup.'

Apprehensive though we might be about David's reaction, it didn't stop either Babs or me going straight off to sleep that night. Too tired even to heat a tin of spaghetti, we'd thrown off our clothes and tumbled into bed.

I must have been too exhausted even to dream and it seemed that I'd been in bed only a few minutes when I was awakened by a commotion of whinnying ponies and banging doors.

'Quick! The pony thieves are back!'

I shook Babs awake before pulling on jeans and a jumper over my pyjamas and hurrying outside.

As we ran towards the stables, a familiar grey shape passed us in the moonlight, almost cannoning into me so that I jumped aside, pushing Babs against the wall.

'Misty!' I groaned as I dashed after my pony. 'You wretch! Come back.'

It was useless, of course, to call; and, even as Babs and I ran after her, we were overtaken by the plumply bulging forms of three of the dark-coloured fell brood mares, all heading in the same direction towards the stableyard.

'What's going on here?' came David's voice from a window of the farmhouse.

Next moment the yard was illuminated as he switched on the outside lights.

In the sudden brightness we saw the door of Saladin's loosebox was open and that the stallion was not inside. In his place Misty and

Patch were greedily pulling at his hay net while the three brood mares jostled for a share.

From the adjacent looseboxes, came the crash and bang of hooves as Centaur and Ebony kicked their doors and mangers, protesting at being left out of the feast.

'Good grief! I might have known it!' As he raced across the yard, David rounded angrily on Babs and me. 'Can't you even be trusted to fasten the gate of your own ponies' field?' He clapped a hand to his head. 'Sarah was right. I ought to have had more sense than to let you stay here without Carol to keep an eye on you.'

'That's not fair,' Babs flashed over her shoulder, tugging at Patch's head-collar to get him away from the hay net. 'It wasn't Jackie and me who left the gate open. It must have been the pony thieves.'

'Pony thieves!' David scoffed in scorn. 'As if we haven't heard enough of that nonsense! But I suppose any excuse will do to hide your own inefficiency and carelessness.'

Dragging Misty out of the loosebox, I took a deep breath before facing him. 'If there weren't any pony thieves, David, how do you think Saladin's box came to be empty in the first place? He couldn't have opened the door himself.'

'Saladin!' David groaned as the full meaning of the disaster struck him. 'Of course, he's missing now – roaming goodness knows where over the countryside.' Tight-lipped with anger he looked from Babs to me. 'You two girls and your ponies are an out-and-out menace.'

'I quite agree.' Calm in her corded jeans and emerald sweater, Sarah had emerged to take her employer's part. 'Carol ought to have had more sense than to invite Babs and Jackie here in the first place. As it is, why not phone her parents to collect them first thing in the morning?'

'Hey, hang on a minute! We don't know that it is Babs and Jackie who are to blame!' Tarquin's hair was spiky from sleep and he was agitatedly wiping his glasses as he stooped to examine something lying on the ground. 'I admit I don't know much about stable management but I do remember reading somewhere that it was an old trick to lure away horses and ponies with aniseed— '

'Aniseed?' David looked at him as if he was out of his mind. 'What are you drivelling about, Tarquin? What on earth has aniseed got to do with it?'

'Take no notice,' urged Sarah. 'He's just trying to side-track the issue.'

'No, I'm not,' Tarquin asserted, resuming his spectacles. 'Look!' He pointed to some small dark brown objects amid the trampled mud and straw of the yard. 'Aniseed drops.'

David picked one up and held it under his nose to sniff. 'You're right, Tarquin. These are aniseed.'

'And what does that prove?' Sarah was sceptical.' Only that someone's been eating aniseed sweets and dropped some. Surely it's dog stealers who use aniseed, not pony thieves.'

'Pony thieves and dog thieves, too, Sarah,' Tarquin corrected her. 'I remember that the article I read mentioned both.'

'So that explains how the thieves were able to get Saladin away without him squealing blue murder and savaging them. They lured him with aniseed.' David moved towards the house. 'I'm going to call the police right away. That stallion's worth a great deal of money.'

CHAPTER TEN

DIAL 999!

'Half of David's capital's sunk into Saladin,' Tarquin explained as his brother followed by Sarah, headed indoors. 'The stallion cost as much as all the brood mares put together.' In that lit-up stableyard the eyes behind his glasses seemed to blink at Babs and me. 'That's why you two mustn't mind his not waiting to apologise for misjudging you. Take it from me, he'll be only too ready to make his peace with you both in the morning, but just now he's too much on his mind. He's apt to fly off the handle in the heat of the moment, is my half-brother, but he's a fair-minded chap for all that.'

Tarquin stayed to help Babs and me return Misty, Patch and the three brood mares to their field.

Drenching rain began to fall as we tugged, pushed and slapped the reluctant animals to get them away from the treasure-trove of Saladin's loosebox. Already the hay net was slack, and one of the mares was questing the ground for any stray oats that might have drifted from the stallion's muzzle, while Patch was munching the bedding straw.

'Come on, you greedy pony!' Worried about the stolen Saladin and exasperated by Patch's behaviour, Babs was near tears as she pulled at the skewbald's head-collar. 'Jackie, leave Misty for a moment and give me a hand. Talk about an immovable object. Ouch!' She yelled as I put my weight against Patch's quarters. 'Now he's standing on my foot.' She turned to Tarquin. 'It's at times like these that I wonder why I ever became a pony-girl.'

Eventually, wet and weary, we managed to get the five ponies out of the yard and drive them along the lane to the field.

'I wonder how this came to be open.' Babs examined the catch of the gate in mystification as the last of the brood mares ambled through. 'It's a pull-back latch,' she demonstrated. 'So none of the ponies could have nosed it up themselves. Not even Patch!'

'We must blame the thieves,' I reasoned. 'Probably they let out the ponies intentionally, knowing they would create a disturbance that would cover their getting Saladin away.'

'But surely,' Tarquin reasoned, 'if it was the thieves who let the ponies out they'd have taken them along, too. They must have had a vehicle for Saladin, and a full load would have been more profitable than a half-empty truck.'

'A truck!' exclaimed Babs. 'Clutterbuck's livestock removals! Remember?' She tied the gate with a halter rope to reinforce the catch before turning towards the house. 'We must remind David to tell the police about Redbeard and the driver. They may have taken Saladin to the Clutterbucks' depot at Black Water.'

'Hang on a minute!' Tarquin stooped to retrieve something from the ground. 'One of you has dropped a scarf. It's a bit muddy, I'm afraid, but it will wash.'

'A scarf!' Babs shone her torch on to the wisp of emerald chiffon he was holding. 'That's not mine.' She shook her head. 'Nor yours, Jackie, is it?' She turned to me.

'No.' I gazed at the muddied chiffon. Where had I seen a scarf like that? Of course, I remembered. 'It's Sarah's.'

'Then what's it doing here?' Tarquin puzzled. 'It was lying right inside the gate.'

'Which means Sarah must have been in the

field and dropped it after we put Misty and Patch in this evening,' Babs said slowly.

'Oh, no!' I gasped, horrified as I realised where my cousin's train of thought might be leading. 'I'm sure Sarah wouldn't have had anything to do with stealing Saladin, would she?'

'I'm not thinking that she did,' Babs stretched out her hand for the scarf. 'Sarah probably opened the ponies' gate so that they'd get out and we'd land in trouble with David. It was just her bad luck that she mistimed it to coincide with a visit from the pony thieves.'

I looked at Tarquin. 'Is that what you think?'

'It's possible,' Tarquin said reluctantly. 'I can't quite size Sarah up. She's efficient with the horses, and that's what David needs, but I must confess she never seemed to hit it off with Carol. She seemed to go out of her way to annoy her in fact.'

'See what I mean?' Babs turned to me. 'Tarquin noticed it, too. It isn't just my imagination. Sarah dislikes us because she's jealous of Carol.'

'Jealous of Carol?' Tarquin turned the idea over in his mind. 'That could be it, I suppose. After all Carol's had a lot of advantages that Sarah hasn't— '

'Including catching your half-brother's fancy,'

86

Babs pointed out romantically. She pulled up the outsize polo collar of her jersey to shield her head. 'Come on. Let's run to the house. It's raining stair rods, and we must remind David to tell the police about the Clutterbucks' truck.'

Twenty minutes later we were drying out in front of the farmhouse Aga while Sarah heated cocoa on the top. A police constable sat at the table taking notes about Saladin's disappearance while, outside, his mate radioed from the patrol car to alert headquarters to investigate the Clutterbuck premises at Black Water.

Neither Babs nor Tarquin nor I had said anything to David or the police about the finding of the emerald scarf, but Babs had hung it conspicuously over the Aga rail to dry and once or twice I thought I had caught Sarah glancing at it apprehensively.

'You say you've seen this fellow with the red beard previously, Miss?' Pencil poised, the note-taking constable looked questioningly at Babs, who nodded.

'Yes. I saw him up on the fell two days ago when we arrived. He had a black-and-white dog with him and he was driving three ponies. The ponies were trotting up the hillside in front of us and then they suddenly disappeared. We couldn't understand it.'

Sarah glanced sceptically at the policeman. 'Just a trick of the mist, don't you think, Constable?'

A flicker of a smile twitched the young policeman's lips. 'Touch of the Ghost Ponies of Borrow Fell, perhaps,' he said jokingly.

David's glance quelled him. 'I think we've got to treat this matter seriously, Constable, don't you? I must remind you that a valuable thoroughbred stallion and a pedigree brood mare – over two thousand pounds worth of stock – are missing.'

'To say nothing of Mr Wellfield's pony,' put in Tarquin firmly. 'If thieves took my half-brother's stallion, then it's only reasonable to believe that our neighbour's missing mare was stolen, too.'

'Quite.' The constable wrote busily.

Ten minutes later his fellow policeman came in from the car. 'One of our mobile patrol cars has been over to Black Water. There are no signs of any horses at Clutterbucks' depot, and the keyholder says he doesn't know of any tall young man with a red beard.' He looked at Babs. 'Mind you, they do have a number of drivers, and it's possible one of them might have a friend answering to that description. One of our officers will be going over in the morning to question them.'

So we had to leave it at that. David told Babs and me to go back to the cottage with Sarah, warning us to get what sleep we could for the rest of the night because we would have to continue the search next morning.

'Aren't you going to take your scarf?' Babs challenged Sarah as we left the kitchen.

'Oh yes,' Sarah whipped the wisp of green chiffon from the Aga rail, brushing off the mud with her hand as she turned to the door.

'Don't you want to know where we found it?' I took my cue from Babs, as we crossed the yard.

'Somewhere around the stables, I suppose,' Sarah said casually. 'I remember thinking last night when I was getting ready for bed that I must have dropped it. She looped it casually round her neck. 'Thanks for bringing it in.'

'And thank you, too, Sarah, for letting out our ponies.' Clicking on the cottage light, Babs glared at her across the sitting room. 'We know it's you who was responsible, because Tarquin found your scarf inside the gateway of the field.'

A spasm of uneasiness flitted across Sarah's

face, but next moment she was in control of herself again.

'Nonsense!' She looked challengingly from Babs to me. 'Try telling that to David and you'll be sent packing for sure. It all ties up with your other behaviour. All you're capable of, the pair of you, is making mischief. I suppose it never occurred to either of you that I dropped my scarf when I was checking that the ponies were safe before I came to bed. You wouldn't give me the credit for that, would you? Oh, no, you prefer to think the worst, spoiled pair of pony brats that you are!'

CHAPTER ELEVEN

QUEST FOR A PONY

'Where shall we start looking?'

Rain dripped from Babs's cap on to the collar of her riding mac as she hoisted herself into Patch's saddle.

'Goodness knows.' David paused to pull up Centaur's girth before withdrawing his head from the saddle flap to answer. 'Your guess is as good as mine. The police haven't been able to find any trace of Saladin and the ponies in the premises of any local dealer; so presumably they may still be in the neighbourhood of the farm.'

'Unless they've been driven over the Pennines, or to Scotland,' Sarah pointed out.

'If they have, the police may still be able to find them,' Tarquin said. 'All other police forces will have been alerted by this time. Saladin's a well-known animal. His picture will be in all the papers tonight. Someone will be sure to recognise him.'

'I wouldn't bank on that.' Sarah's eyes flashed green, and I had a disquieting feeling that she did not want Saladin to be recovered. Why? Was she so jealous of David's interest in Carol that she wanted him to be hurt in retaliation? 'Horses can be disguised, you know.'

'Dyed to change their colour?' Babs looked sceptical. 'Who has been seeing too much television now?'

'Oh, stop bickering!' David put his foot into Centaur's stirrup and struggled to mount as the grey circled. 'Just get out and start looking, that's all I ask.'

Piqued, Sarah clapped her legs to Bryony's sides and cantered away through the open gate. David's mouth tightened as he watched her go. Then he turned to the rest of us.

'Right. See you back here at twelve-thirty to compare notes.'

'Agreed.' Tarquin shortened Romany's reins as he looked questioningly across at Babs and me. 'Have you two decided on a line of your own to follow, or are you going to throw in your lot with me?'

'Why not?' I shrugged. 'As none of us has

any idea where to start looking we might as well all three be clueless together.'

'All! But I'm not clueless.' Tarquin looked mysterious. 'In fact I've had the beginnings of an idea.'

'What is it?' In spite of the rain that was running down her face and making wet spikes of her hair, Babs looked agog. 'Do you mean to say that you know where Saladin and the ponies might be, and yet you're holding out on us?'

'Well, it is only an idea.' Tarquin turned Romany towards the gate that led to the fells. 'I didn't want to occupy too many of us with it in case I turned out to be wrong, so it is just as well that David and Sarah are looking for clues elsewhere.'

'Do tell us where we're going!' I put Misty into a canter beside Romany as we pelted up the sodden hillside.

'Borrow Fell,' Tarquin said shortly, driving Romany on with his heels as she shied at a patch of bracken.

'I got the idea last night when you were telling the police constable about your "ghost ponies".'

'Great minds think alike!' Babs called out when half-an-hour later we caught sight of Graham

Wellfield through the driving rain on Borrow Fell.

'Hey, Graham! Wait for us,' I shouted as I urged Misty up the slope towards the stony track on the ridge along which Graham on Heather Damson was trotting. 'If you're on the lookout for ghost ponies, too, don't tell me there's no such thing as telepathy!'

'There isn't.' Graham laughed as he reined up. He shook his dark head like a seal to throw back a lock of rain-drenched hair from his eyes.

'Then how do you come to be here?' asked Babs. 'It's too much of a coincidence that your search should bring you to exactly the same spot as ours.'

Graham nodded towards Tarquin. 'Ask him,' he said with a wink.

'It's simple.' Tarquin paused to wipe the rain drops from his spectacle lenses. 'When you two girls were busy helping David and Sarah out, I took the opportunity to telephone Graham. We put our heads together over the wires. Graham agreed it was time someone investigated the myth of the disappearing "ghost ponies" of Borrow Fell, and here we are.'

'It's a long shot, of course,' said Graham, 'but it is just possible there may be some kind of hiding place up here where the "ghost ponies" are taken. After all, the red-bearded man whom Babs saw was real enough, particularly if, as Tarquin told me, you both saw him again last evening in Kendal. Three ponies, a man and a dog don't just vanish into thin air.'

'Even allowing for the fact that it was misty at the time,' added Tarquin. 'And in any case Jackie and Babs said that the cloud had drifted away . . .'

'It had,' I nodded. 'The sun was shining.'

'Quite.' Tarquin took command. 'We'll ride slowly along the path in single file. You lead, Babs, and stop when you come to the spot where you saw the ponies.'

'If I can find it.' Babs rode Patch forward into the slanting rain. 'I can't see far because of the rain.'

'You can see the lake,' I pointed out. 'That gives you something to go by.'

With my cousin peering round through the driving rain, we rode our ponies along the stony path. Babs was in front of me with Patch's brown-and-white quarters and silky white tail swinging just ahead of Misty as it had done on the day of our arrival when we had thought ourselves lost in the mist.

Suddenly, to the left, I saw a wind-shorn clump of gorse and my mind switched back.

The three ponies had passed behind just such a clump on the day of our arrival before they disappeared.

'It was just about here.' Babs reined up and the rain dripped from her sleeve as she pointed up the hillside.

'Well done!' Tarquin motioned to us to gather round him. 'Somewhere here there may be a hidden building, or even a cave . . .'

'The fells are riddled with caves,' said Graham, 'but I thought I knew most of those in this district. If there is a cave hereabouts, the entrance must be well hidden. However, here goes.'

He turned his pony's head to the right and, fanning out as we went, we walked our mounts slowly forward. Our eyes followed every curve of the ground. We looked behind each bush or tree and into every hollow.

Presently a shout from Babs made us canter towards her. She had dismounted and was halfway up a steep slope where the grass gave way to rocks and a peak towered behind. In front of her was a huge boulder and beyond it we could just see a dark shadow that might be an opening in the mountainside.

Wet rocks made the way slippery, so we jumped down from our ponies and, pulling our reins over their heads, led them to where Babs was standing. As we did so Misty blew loudly. Then we heard an answering whinny from inside the cave.

'Eureka!' Tarquin's glasses were misted with rain and his face was pink with excitement. 'I do believe we've found them.'

'Steady, everyone.' Graham dismounted and handed his reins to me. 'If the ponies and Saladin are in the cave, the thieves may be with them. We don't want a show-down with Saladin savaging someone, and perhaps some of the ponies getting hurt. Wait here, all of you.'

We held our breaths, terrified that one of our ponies might answer the whinny that had come from the cave, but fortunately our mounts were all too breathless from the canter up the fellside to call.

My heart was thumping against my ribs and as I looked across to Babs I could tell that she was almost choking with suppressed excitement and fear. Only Tarquin seemed calm.

We waited for what seemed like ages. Then came the sound of Graham's footsteps returning from the interior of the cave.

'Well?' I could see that Babs could not keep

back the query as he emerged blinking into the stronger light.

'The thieves seem to have gone, and they've taken Saladin and Greyling with them. Elderberry's here, though.'

'Just Elderberry?' I asked, disappointed.

'Not exactly – no.' Graham's voice sounded strangely awed. 'I think you'd better knot the ponies' reins and leave them outside. Then you can come into the cave and see for yourselves.'

CHAPTER TWELVE

A SURPRISE IN THE CAVE

Fetlock deep in cut bracken, Elderberry faced us watchfully from the far end of the cave. Behind her we could see something dark and rounded.

As we gazed, the shape moved, extending spindly forelegs. Head raised, small ears flicking, Elderberry's foal regarded us alertly.

'How wonderful!' I said in a whisper. 'What a little beauty.'

'Miraculous!' breathed Babs.

But Tarquin was looking past the foal and its mother to a pile of unused bracken in the corner of the cave. Beside stood a broken bale of hay and a half-empty sack of pony nuts. Behind his glasses, I could almost see Tarquin's mind working.

'The thieves must have brought Elderberry here,' he said at last.

'There were other animals here, too.' He stepped forward to remove some grey pony hairs that had rubbed off against a jutting piece of rock. He turned to Graham. 'Didn't you say that your missing pony was a grey?'

Graham nodded, and I saw his gaze travel to the trampled floor of the cave. He moved forward, stooping to peer more closely at the hoofprints.

I'd say there were several unshod ponies here as well as a bigger animal, wearing shoes.'

'That would be Saladin!' Babs exclaimed.

'But where are they all now?' I wondered aloud. 'And why did the thieves leave?'

Tarquin shook his head. 'I've no idea; unless, of course, they were disturbed.'

'That figures,' said Graham. 'If the thieves had to leave in a hurry, Elderberry and the foal would have hindered them too much.'

'Probably they left on foot,' reasoned Babs. 'Otherwise they would have taken the hay and the pony nuts.'

Tarquin took off his spectacles and wiped them abstractedly as if lost in thought. 'What I ask myself, is how the thieves brought the feed up in the first place?'

'On the back of a pony, I suppose,' Graham said. 'It wouldn't be too difficult.'

'Does it matter?' Babs demanded. 'Does any of it matter, except that Elderberry and her darling foal are safe and the others are still missing?'

'Saladin and the others can't have been taken far,' I pointed out, 'unless, of course, the thieves drove them to a truck . . .'

'In which case they might be halfway to some dock or other.' Tarquin groaned. He turned towards the rest of us. 'I think I should ride back to Singing Waters to alert the police as to what we've found while you three scour the mountainside for clues.' He turned to Graham. 'Will Elderberry and the foal be all right here on their own?'

Graham looked doubtful. 'Someone should stay. I don't think there's much chance of the thieves coming back, but there's always the risk of a dog, or a sheep, or some other animal getting in here and upsetting the mare.'

'You stay with her, Graham,' said Babs. 'You know far more about ponies than any of us. Jackie and I will carry on searching for clues.'

Graham glanced at Tarquin, who nodded his confirmation of the plan. 'Right you are, then. Will do!'

We hadn't been searching long when Babs

spotted a muddle of hoof marks where a climber's track crossed the mountainside. Among the smaller indentations of unshod pony hooves was the unmistakable imprint of a large, shod foot – Saladin's!

'They went this way.' My cousin touched the flagging Patch with her heels urging him along the muddy path at a canter.

Misty pulled at her bit to follow. Perhaps she thought we were going home. Anything, no doubt, would seem better to her than the endless slow questing in the steadily dripping rain which had darkened her coat with wetness and settled in heavy droplets on her mane.

Disregarding the water that ran down my neck, my heart filled with hope at the sight of the hoofprints. How wonderful it would be if we were able to track down Saladin and the Wellfields' pony before the thieves had time to load them into a truck.

The hoof marks led straight along the path that climbed to the saddle of the mountain. So, up we cantered with Babs in the lead.

Suddenly, my cousin reined up and I had to halt Misty so sharply on the muddy surface that her hooves skidded beneath her.

'Look!' Babs pointed through the driving rain to the road down below in the valley. There we could see a blue van drawn up while three men in dark waterproof clothing had spread out to cover the hillside. 'The police!'

'Gosh!' I exclaimed. 'So that's why the thieves did a bolt with Saladin and the ponies. They must have got wind that justice was on their trail.'

Babs and I cupped our hands to our mouths to call to the policemen. We wanted to tell them that we had found the ponies' tracks but the wind only snatched our voices and hurled them back against the mountainside.

'It's no good.' Babs shortened her reins to turn Patch. 'I'll have to ride down to the police and tell them that they're looking in the wrong direction.' She clapped her legs into the skewbald's sides yelling over her shoulder to me. 'Carry on following the trail, Jackie. I'll catch up as soon as I can.'

Taking a short cut, I galloped Misty across the turf. When I rejoined the path on the crest of the hill, a heart-stopping sight lay before me. Down below, at the head of the valley, was a small reservoir that served one of the farms. Now, to my horror, I saw that the dam wall had broken and the water was pouring down the valley in a torrent, flooding a broad hollow so that a tree-crowned hillock in the middle formed an islet. There, marooned upon it and looking like toy farmyard animals from this height, were four ponies and a horse. One of the ponies looked like the Wellfields' missing grey. The others were dark like the mares that had seemed to disappear into the mountainside on the day of our arrival. Even from this distance I could see the horse was David's missing chestnut stallion – Saladin!

As I watched the ripples washed higher and higher. Each moment now the island was shrinking as the flood of water from the broken dam encroached. If the ponies and Saladin were not rescued they would soon be engulfed. They would be swept away as the stream spilled into the lower valley. They would be dashed against the rocks and drowned.

I did not know what I could do to prevent the tragedy. There was no clear idea in my head as I urged Misty down the steep slope towards the swirling torrent.

The mountainside was slippery and sodden. Below us was a rocky scree. I could only lean forward over Misty's neck, keeping my weight off her hocks while I drove her on with my legs until, finally, she was almost sitting on her haunches to slide.

Below us the four mares clustered nearer

to the stallion. They were looking to him for leadership as the water crept closer.

'Saladin!' I called, hoping to encourage him to come through the flooding water to me, and so give the ponies a lead before it became too deep for them to wade.

I saw the stallion's chestnut ears prick. There was no doubt that he had heard my voice, but all he would do was look nervously at the torrent and back higher up the tree-clad knoll.

There was nothing for it but for me to go to him.

CHAPTER THIRTEEN

MISTY TO THE RESCUE

My pony put back her ears and dug in her toes
as the flood water washed nearer.

'Come on, girl. You've got to do it. We can't
let Saladin and the ponies drown. We must
reach them, somehow.'

Misty was trembling, but I drove her on with
my heels. Her nostrils flared red and her eyes
were rolling as she entered the water.

The flood swirled round her fetlocks, then
it reached her knees. Frightened, she snorted
and tried to back. Saladin neighed to her from
the island and, afraid though she was, the
stallion's call steadied her, and it seemed as
though she had to obey. She went, deeper
and deeper into the water until at last she was
swimming.

I shortened my reins to keep Misty's head
high as she churned forward, realising that the

current would tend to carry her down-river, I pointed her nose towards a spot well above the island.

Thankfully I felt her feet touch solid ground. Whinnying, she surged ashore to join Saladin and the pony mares. The Wellfields' grey tried jealously to nip her, and Saladin threw up his head and snorted, but the other three mares were quiet. Now and then they shifted nervously as the water lapped nearer.

Turning Misty, I tried to round them up. I wanted to drive them to swim across the flooded valley to safety, but they would not go. They scattered and crowded together again round Saladin on the higher ground.

There was only one thing for it. Somehow Saladin would have to give a lead. I rode Misty alongside the stallion and reached to grasp his mane.

'Come on, old boy. Do your stuff and show the ladies the way.'

Saladin would not move. His eyes rolled as I pulled at his mane. Next moment, his head snaked round and I had to twist aside in the saddle to escape his teeth.

What was I to do? Turning Misty, I tried riding at the stallion from behind.

'Go on, boy! Saladin, go on!'

I struck him across the quarters with my switch, but he stood as motionless and immovable as a rock. Meanwhile the flood water washed nearer and nearer. It was halfway up the ponies' legs and I felt desperate. Unless I could get the stallion to lead them into swimming ashore, the probability was that they would panic and be drowned.

There was only one thing left to try. Knowing Saladin's reputation as a difficult stallion, a potential killer, I was terrified, but I knew that somehow I would have to get on his back and ride him through the flood myself.

I did not like abandoning Misty. It seemed like treachery to separate from my precious pony and leave her to swim ashore by herself, but I thought she would follow Saladin. Knotting her reins so that she could not catch her feet in their trailing loops, I kicked my feet free of the stirrups and again rode her alongside, tensing myself in order to spring on to the stallion's back.

To this day, I don't know how I managed it, but one minute I was half-kneeling on Misty's saddle and the next I was scrambling on to the tall chestnut. Saladin snorted and laid back his ears, but I patted his neck and tried to speak calmly to him.

'There's no need to be afraid. Come on!'

I drove him on with my heels.

Eyes rolling, he moved forward cautiously into the water, step by step until he was shoulder-deep. Suddenly he stopped, and looked round doubtfully. I touched him with my switch and urged him on with my calves, but he would not move. The water was now up to his neck and he was trembling. I looked back to see Misty and the other pony mares hesitating behind us. Their feet were still on solid ground but the water was well up their chests.

'Saladin, you must move, boy! Go on! Please, go on!'

I dug my heels into him, but he only began to tremble even more violently. He had lost his nerve, and I knew that he would shortly begin to panic.

I don't know what the outcome would have been but, at that fateful moment, two riders came into view on the shoulder of the opposite hill – David and Babs. Centaur, the grey stallion that David was riding, threw up his head and called.

Hearing him, Misty and the other mares surged forward into the deeper water and started to swim strongly towards him. Then, making up his mind, Saladin plunged after them. A few short thrusts of his powerful shoulders and we were through the worst of the flood and wading ashore after the mares.

David and Babs, on the backs of Centaur and Patch, slithered down the slope towards us. Behind them, three policemen were scrambling down the scree.

As I swung my leg over Saladin's back and slid to the ground, I found my legs shaking. I started to shiver and, when David and Babs rode up, my teeth were chattering so much that I could hardly speak.

'Well done, Jackie! Well done!' David slid down from Centaur and put his jacket around me.

'Steady, miss.' The strong arm of one of the policemen went about me as my legs started to buckle.

Two of the constables hoisted me on to Patch's back, while Babs led Misty and David took charge of Saladin. The other policeman mounted Centaur. The pony mares trotted beside us as we began the journey to the parked police car, where a fourth policeman was in radio contact with headquarters, alerting the sergeant about the broken dam, so that any persons whose property, or stock, lay in the path of the flood, could be warned.

*   *   *

'Hurry up, Jackie!' Babs hammered on the bathroom door an hour and a half later as I lay soaking in the hot bath which David had recommended to drive out the chill. 'Get dressed and come down to the kitchen. I've made some hot cocoa, and I've a whole lot of news.'

My cousin's voice was full of suppressed excitement, so I heaved myself reluctantly out of the blissful warmth, hastily dried, and with the towel round me padded to the bedroom to put on dry jeans and my thickest sweater.

Babs's eyes were sensational as she poured out the hot drinks.

'Graham's father has been here to identify their mare. He says the police think the pony which you rescued from the bog is one of three stolen from a Yorkshire breeder. A local farmer has claimed one of the others, and now Mr Wellfield's gone up to Borrow Fell to bring down Elderberry and the foal. Saladin's so upset that David can't leave him.'

My cousin was already breathless from relating her news, but, even so, there was still more to come. She eyed me speculatively. 'Have you noticed anything different about the cottage yet?'

'Different about the cottage, Babs?' I looked at her in bewilderment. 'What on earth do you mean?'

'Anything missing, for instance,' Babs prompted.

I glanced round. Now that my cousin had mentioned it, I realised that a red glass horse of Sarah's had gone from the kitchen window-ledge. Sarah's radio was also missing. Her gumboots were not in their customary corner and her fun-fur jacket was missing from its hook behind the door.

'Have we been burgled?' I asked. 'Or—?'

Babs nodded. 'Sarah's gone,' she announced dramatically. 'When David sent you across for a hot bath and I went with Tarquin to dry Centaur, we found Bryony in one of the loose-boxes. Sarah's wet tack was in the saddle room and her motor scooter was missing. I looked in her room just now while you were in the bath, and her clothes have gone, too. Everything, suitcase and all! She's made a total clear-out. The drawers and wardrobe are as empty as if she had never been.'

I could hardly take it in.

'Why?' I puzzled. 'Why would a girl like Sarah go off at a time of crisis, just when she was needed most?'

'Why indeed?' Babs's eyebrows rose. 'You may well ask yourself that, Jackie, particularly if you recall that we found Sarah's scarf in the ponies' field, just after Misty and Patch had been turned loose in the middle of the night to create chaos so that the thieves could get Saladin away unnoticed! Guilt! That's why she's gone.'

CHAPTER FOURTEEN

DAVID'S BIG NEWS

'We shall have to report this to David,' Babs decided. 'Come on.'

As we crossed the yard to Saladin's loosebox we saw Tarquin standing by the door talking to David who was inside with the stallion. Tarquin looked round as we approached but David went on talking quietly to Saladin and pulling his ears.

'I can guess what you've come to say,' Tarquin told us. 'But I've already told David that Sarah's missing.'

'Worse than that,' I said. 'She seems to have taken all her belongings with her.'

Saladin moved restlessly in the deep straw, and a fresh patch of sweat darkened the satiny chestnut of his neck. 'Wherever Sarah may have gone, there's nothing we can do about it.' David rolled back the rug from the stallion's quarters and reached for the wisp to dry him off again. 'I can't leave this fellow until he's completely calmed down. So there's no question of driving after Sarah in the car, and I don't feel inclined to tell the police . . .'

'Not even if she's in with the thieves?' Tarquin queried.

'Not even then,' David said decisively. 'We don't know all the facts, so we can't judge. Sarah may have a sharp tongue but, up to now, she's always worked well. And she's had a hard life, you know. Her father was a very rough diamond. He went to prison once for horse doping. Sarah told me that when I took her on. She made no effort to conceal it, said she wanted to put it all behind her.'

'But perhaps she hasn't,' said Babs.

'Perhaps not.' David looked at her sharply across Saladin's back. 'But, even then, I don't want to know. Pressure may have been put on her by someone outside.'

'Someone from her past?' Tarquin picked up his brother's thought. 'I can see the way your mind's working. However, suppose we let Sarah go free and she continues working in with the pony thieves.

Haven't we a responsibility to other pony owners?'

'We've a responsibility to Sarah, too,' David countered. 'Firstly, we don't even know that she did have a hand in the stealing of Saladin. She may have become frightened because of her father's record— '

'And decided to leave in case the police tried to put the blame on her,' I nodded.

'But what about her scarf?' asked Babs. 'How do you account for that being in Misty's and Patch's field?'

'There could be some innocent explanation,' I said.

'Thanks, Jackie.' David looked across at me. 'I'm glad someone agrees with me. Now to take your minds off it, why don't you all three go into Kendal to see Carol? Wednesday afternoon is visiting time, and she'll feel forsaken if no one turns up. Tell you what,' he looked across at Babs and me, 'you two rustle up some sandwiches. Bring some over here to me and meanwhile,' he turned to Tarquin, 'I'll beg a loan of that notebook you carry about with you. If I can get this big silly calmed down— ' he slapped Saladin affectionately, 'I may just manage to scrawl a note, while you're eating your lunch, for you to take to Carol. Visiting starts at half past two, and the bus leaves the end of the lane at two o'clock.'

'Carol was pleased to get your letter, and she sent this in reply.' Babs handed an envelope to David as she, Tarquin and I trooped into the farmhouse kitchen at half past five that afternoon. 'She's allowed up most of the day now and Aunt Di's coming to take her home next Tuesday.'

'She'll be coming back here later, of course,' I added, 'that is, if you still need her. The doctors say she must have a two months' rest, but I know she'll be looking forward to getting back to Singing Waters.'

'I should think so.' David's face looked oddly tense as he drew Carol's letter from the envelope which she had given us.

He turned away to the window as he read it and I remember thinking it was strange that he stood there, gazing at the contents for fully three minutes before he turned back to us with a crinkly kind of smile on his face.

Then, without letting us know what Carol had to say, he turned to the range and brought an appetising-looking dish of baked beans, cheese, onions and tomatoes from the oven.

'Bean bake,' he announced, setting it on the table. 'Saladin quietened down shortly after you'd gone so I thought I'd turn cook and have your tea ready when you got back. I hope it's all right,' he added anxiously, spooning out the helpings on to our eagerly held plates.

We had just finished David's bean bake, voted it delicious, and were about to start on a large dripping cake which Graham had just brought in with his mother's best wishes, when we heard the pop-pop of Sarah's scooter in the courtyard.

Pushing back our chairs, we crowded to the door in time to see her lift off her safety helmet and shake free her auburn hair before walking towards us.

'I don't know whether I'll be welcome or not— ' Her green eyes looked challengingly from one to the other of us before her gaze finally came to rest on David. 'I thought I'd better come back and face the music. They've arrested our Frankie, so there's no point in me trying to hide out . . .' Her shoulders seemed to sag and she looked suddenly defeated.

David put out a hand to steady her, as he turned to the kitchen.

'Come inside, Sarah, and sit down. Then you

can tell us all about it. Jackie, see if there's another cup of tea in the pot.'

As she sipped the hot liquid, Sarah told us what had happened. Apparently the red-bearded man whom we had seen driving the ponies was her older brother, Frankie. She had no idea that he was in the district until she awakened the previous night to hear Misty and Patch whinnying. She had gone out to investigate without wakening Babs and me, only to be nearly knocked down as Patch had galloped past, heading for the stableyard and the feed bins. Before she could pick herself up, her brother had appeared, leading Saladin. She had remonstrated with him, but to no avail. A second man, presumably the driver of the cattle truck whom the police had now apprehended along with Frankie, had held her shoulders while her brother, having fed Saladin aniseed balls to win his co-operation, had sprung on to the stallion's back and headed for the fell.

'Why didn't you tell us this last night?' Babs asked pointedly, still suspicious.

'How could she?' Tarquin as usual could see both sides. 'It would have meant informing on her brother.'

'That's right,' Sarah nodded. 'As a matter

of fact, I didn't know what to do. I knew I owed David loyalty as my employer, but how could I split on Frankie? It would have meant handing my own brother over to the police. You know what they say – blood's thicker than water.' She put down her cup and saucer and got wearily to her feet. 'There now I've told you that, I might as well be off.'

'Where to?' asked David.

'Goodness knows!' She shrugged. 'I suppose I could go home to Dad for a start. He's kept out of trouble for more than two years now, so I dare say we could make a go of things together.'

David stepped in front of her and looked down at her straightly.

'There's no need for you to "make a go of things" anywhere but here, Sarah, if you want to stay.'

She pushed back a strand of damp auburn hair and eyed him doubtfully.

'I'd only be here on sufferance, though, wouldn't I? It would be charity, in a manner of speaking; you'd just be doing your bit to help a near-criminal keep straight.'

'Not at all,' David assured her. 'I need your help. I hope Babs and Jackie will stay on until the end of their school holidays, but they haven't your experience and I shall be short-handed without Carol. Besides, Sarah, you're no "near-criminal" as you put it. The fact that you came back to tell us what happened proves that. I'd be very pleased to have you stay on here as a permanent member of the Singing Waters staff, as long as you can get on with Carol and the others, that is.'

'I'll do that all right, never fear.' Sarah held out her hand to shake his in impulsive gratitude. 'You're a friend, David Browning, and that's for sure. As for you two,' she turned penitently to Babs and me, 'I'm sorry I've been so short-tempered. I'm afraid I was jealous of Carol, but that's all over now.'

'That's good, Sarah.' David's face was happier as he turned to Babs and me. 'Now I can tell you some good news. Your cousin Carol and I are getting engaged.'

'So that's what the notes were all about!' Babs exclaimed. She turned to me excitedly. 'Fancy you and me playing Cupid's messengers!'

'Great news, David!' Tarquin fondly slapped his brother on the back while Graham shook him by the hand. 'The best I've heard for ages!'

For a moment Sarah looked rueful. Then she squared her shoulders and smiled.

'Congratulations, David. I'd like to say that I hope you'll be very happy and to tell you that I think I'm lucky to be able to stay on here to work. I'll do my best for you both.'

'Good for you, Sarah,' I said.

'And good for you, Jackie and Babs,' David smiled. 'You turned out better pony-girls than I'd expected.'

'So you'd let us help again?' Babs angled eagerly.

'Could be.' David wasn't committing himself more than that. 'Could well be!'

Rolf Harris

YOUR CARTOON TIME

Did you know that you can draw?

Rolf Harris shows you how – clearly and
simply – in *Your Cartoon Time*.
Starting with stick figures, he explains how
to develop these step-by-step into your own
stylish characters, and there are ideas too
for how you can use your drawings – as
birthday cards, home movies and so on.

Drawing is fun!

All you need is a pencil, paper and Rolf
Harris's book – *Your Cartoon Time*.

Jean Webster

DADDY-LONG-LEGS

The story of Judy and her mysterious
guardian is one of the most popular romances
ever written, and it has been both filmed and
made into a highly successful musical.
Judy at seventeen is taken from an
Institution, where she is the oldest orphan,
and sent to college – at the expense of an
amused and anonymous Trustee. A
wavering, elongated shadow, once seen, is
her only clue, and this induces her to call
him Daddy-Long-Legs.

Another Knight Book

A Twerp Mystery

THE HEADMASTER WENT SPLAT!

David Tinkler

'Kevin Twerp,' hissed killer Keast, the fer-
ocious headmaster of Shambles School, 'I
want to see you in my room immediately.'
Suddenly, it seemed to go cold. The light
went dim. There was a gasp from the children and the teachers shivered. Kevin felt
faint and his mouth went dry.
Kevin Twerp's life hasn't been easy; pop-
singing dad killed in an air crash, Mum –
Nitty Norah the Hair Explorer – driven out
to work as a school nurse. And, looming,
like a dark shadow, Killer Keast.
But, with the help of WPC Rose Button,
lodger and All-England Mud Wallowing
Champion, things *will* change . . .!

These are the adventures of the famous
Black Stallion and his friend Alec that are
available in Knight

Walter Farley
The Black Stallion
The Black Stallion Revolts
The Black Stallion Returns
The Black Stallion and Satan
Son of the Black Stallion
Black Stallion's Courage
The Black Stallion's Filly
The Black Stallion Mystery
The Black Stallion and Flame
The Black Stallion's Ghost
The Black Stallion's Challenge
The Black Stallion and the Stranger
The Black Stallion Legend
The Young Black Stallion

MORE GREAT BOOKS AVAILABLE
FROM KNIGHT